MR. BADGER AND MRS. FOX #1

THE MEETING

Brigitte LUCIANI & Eve THARLET

Graphic Universe™ • Minneapolis • New York

**Thank you to Chris for the proofreading,
the support, and the patience.
—B.L.**

**Thank you to Nicole R., who agreed with
enthusiasm to check my scribbled drawings and
lettering along with the "li'l foxes" in her class.
—E.T.**

Story by Brigitte Luciani
Art by Eve Tharlet
Translation by Carol Klio Burrell

First American edition published in 2010 by Graphic Universe™.
Published by arrangement with MEDIATOON LICENSING - France.

Monsieur Blaireau et Madame Renarde
1/La rencontre
© DARGAUD 2006 - Tharlet & Luciani
www.dargaud.com

Graphic Universe™
A division of Lerner Publishing Group, Inc.
241 First Avenue North
Minneapolis, MN 55401 U.S.A.

Website address: www.lernerbooks.com

Library of Congress Cataloging-in-Publication Data

Luciani, Brigitte.
The meeting / by Brigitte Luciani ; illustrated by Eve Tharlet.
p.   cm. — (Mr. Badger and Mrs. Fox)
Summary: Having lost their home, a fox and her daughter move in with a
badger and his three children, but when the youngsters throw a big party
hoping to prove that they are incompatible, their plan backfires.
ISBN 978-0-7613-5625-7 (lib. bdg. : alk. paper)
[1. Single-parent families—Fiction. 2. Brothers and sisters—Fiction. 3. Badgers—Fiction.
4. Foxes—Fiction. 5. Toleration—Fiction.] I. Tharlet, Eve, ill. II. Title.
PZ7.L9713Mee 2010
[E]—dc22   2009032617

Manufactured in the United States of America
3 - DP - 3/31/12

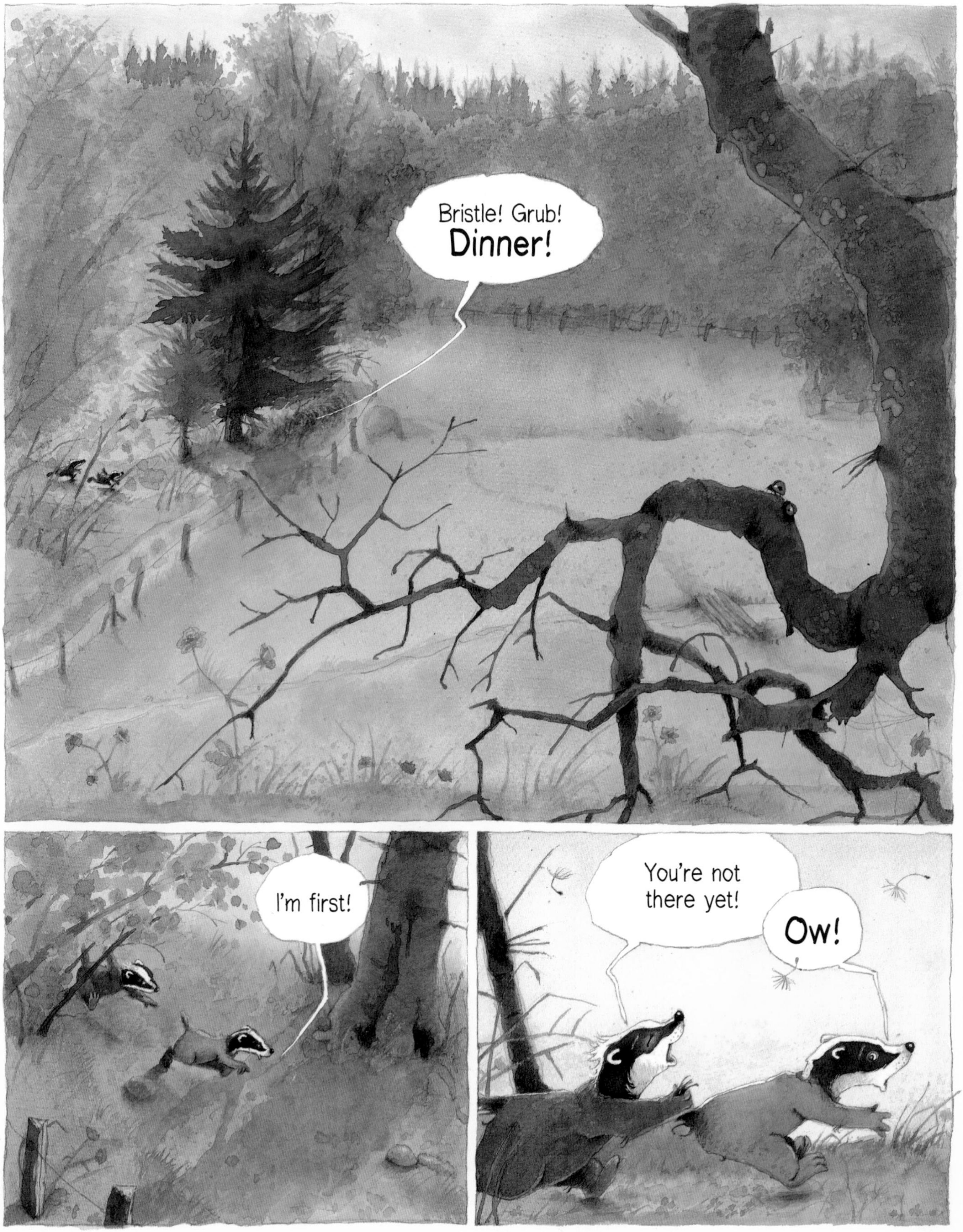
Bristle! Grub! Dinner!
I'm first!
You're not there yet!
Ow!

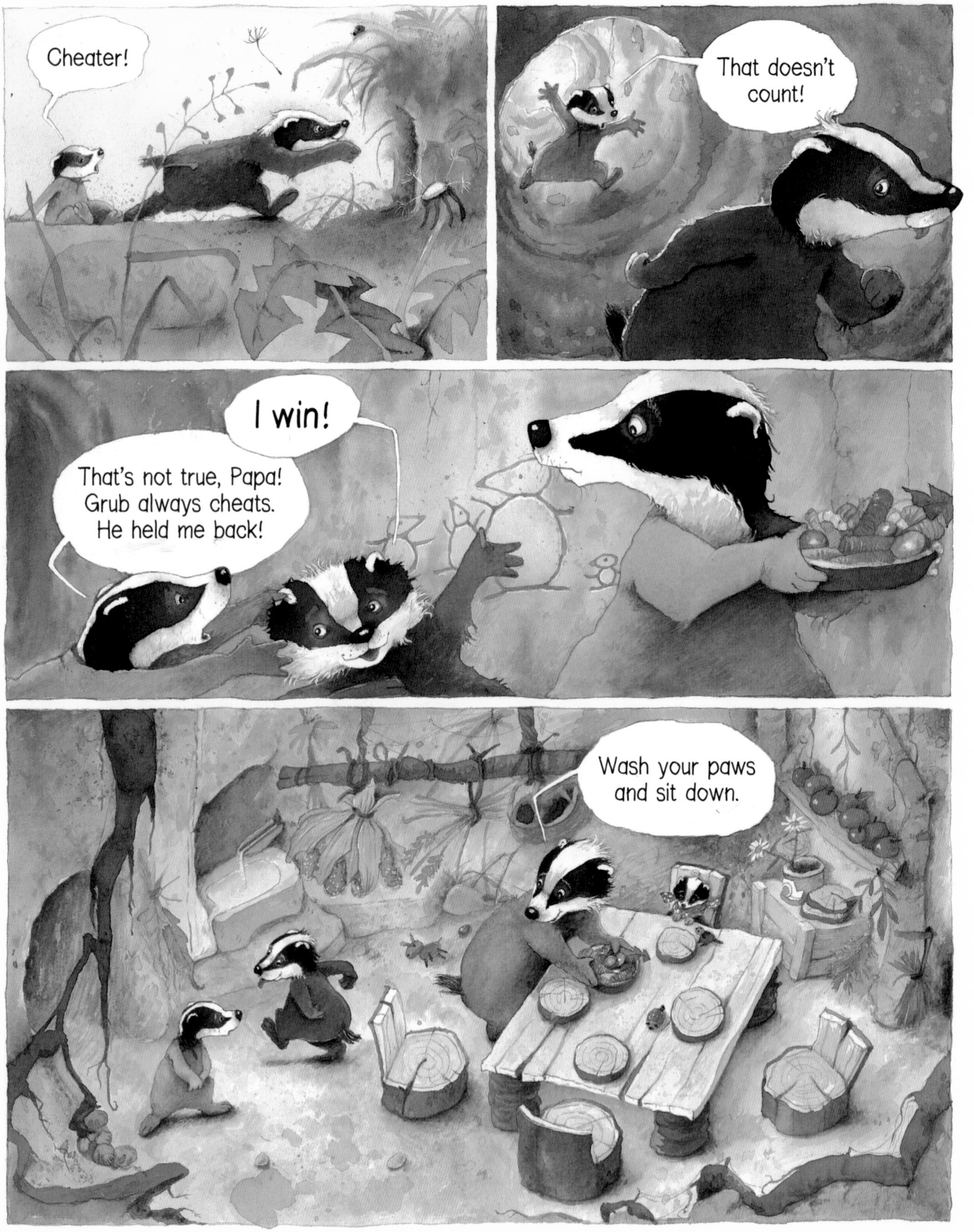
Cheater!
That doesn't count!
I win!
That's not true, Papa! Grub always cheats. He held me back!
Wash your paws and sit down.

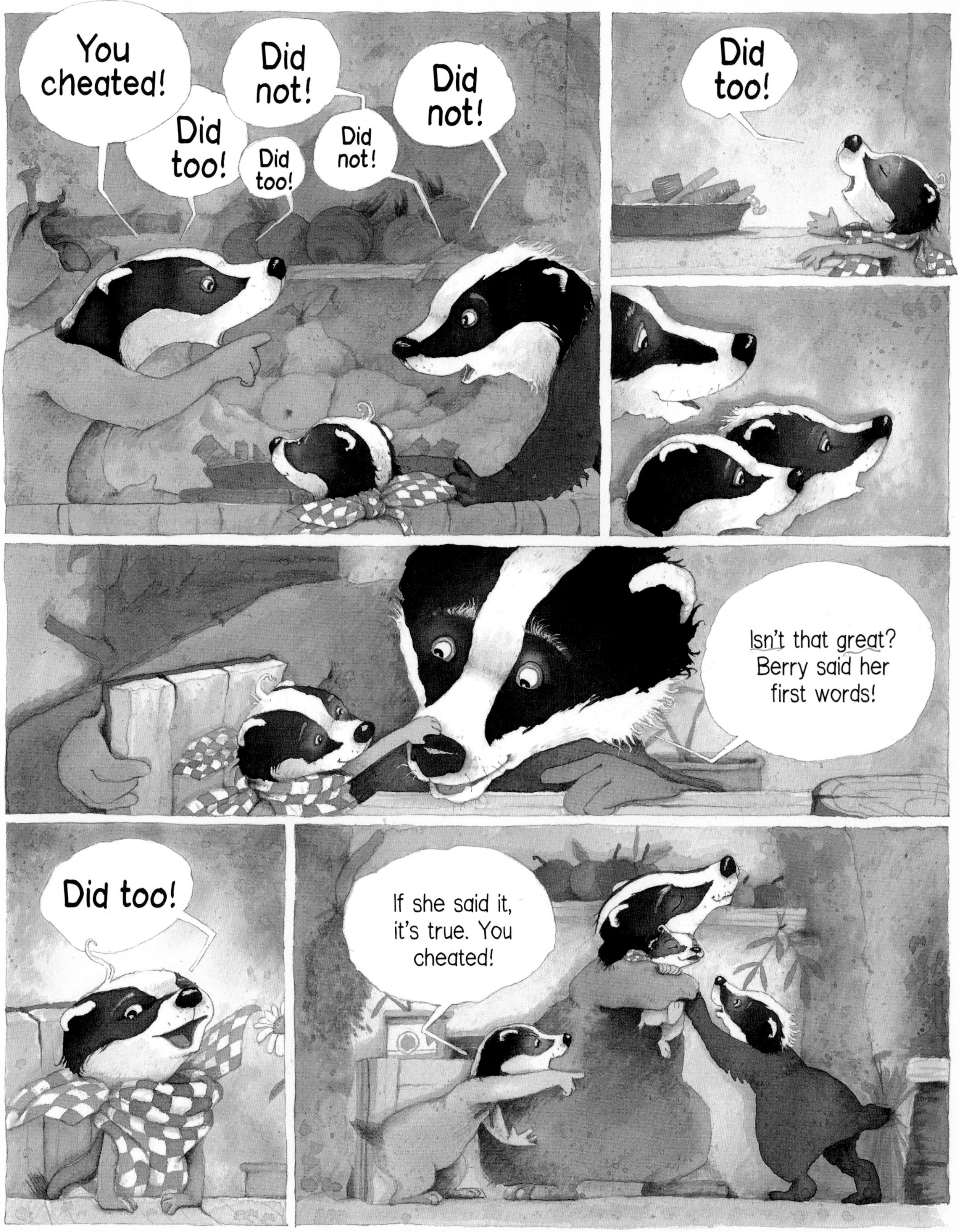
You cheated!
Did not!
Did too!
Did not!
Did too!
Did not!
Did too!
Isn't that great? Berry said her first words!
Did too!
If she said it, it's true. You cheated!

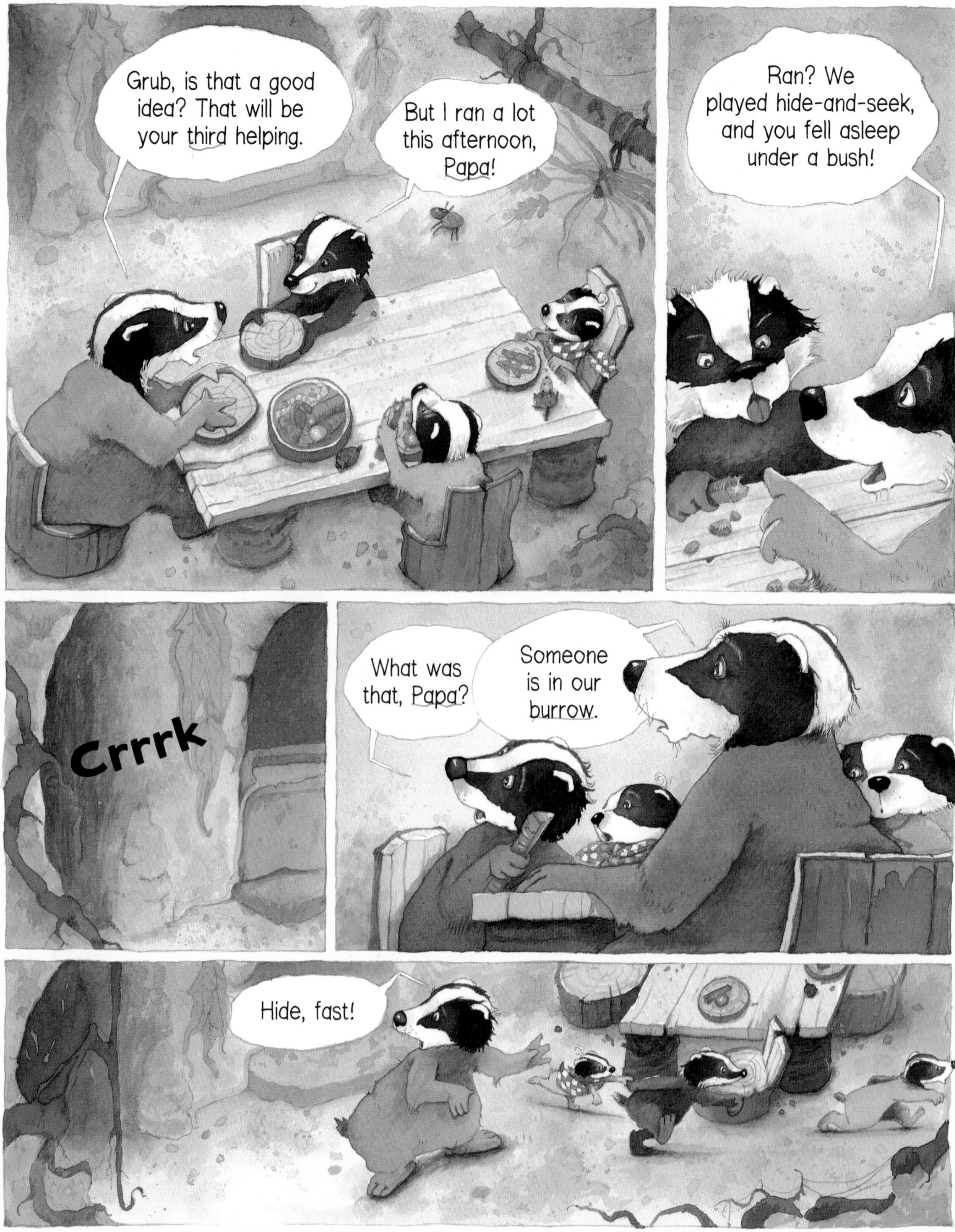
Grub, is that a good idea? That will be your third helping.
But I ran a lot this afternoon, Papa!
Ran? We played hide-and-seek, and you fell asleep under a bush!
Crrrk
What was that, Papa?
Someone is in our burrow.
Hide, fast!

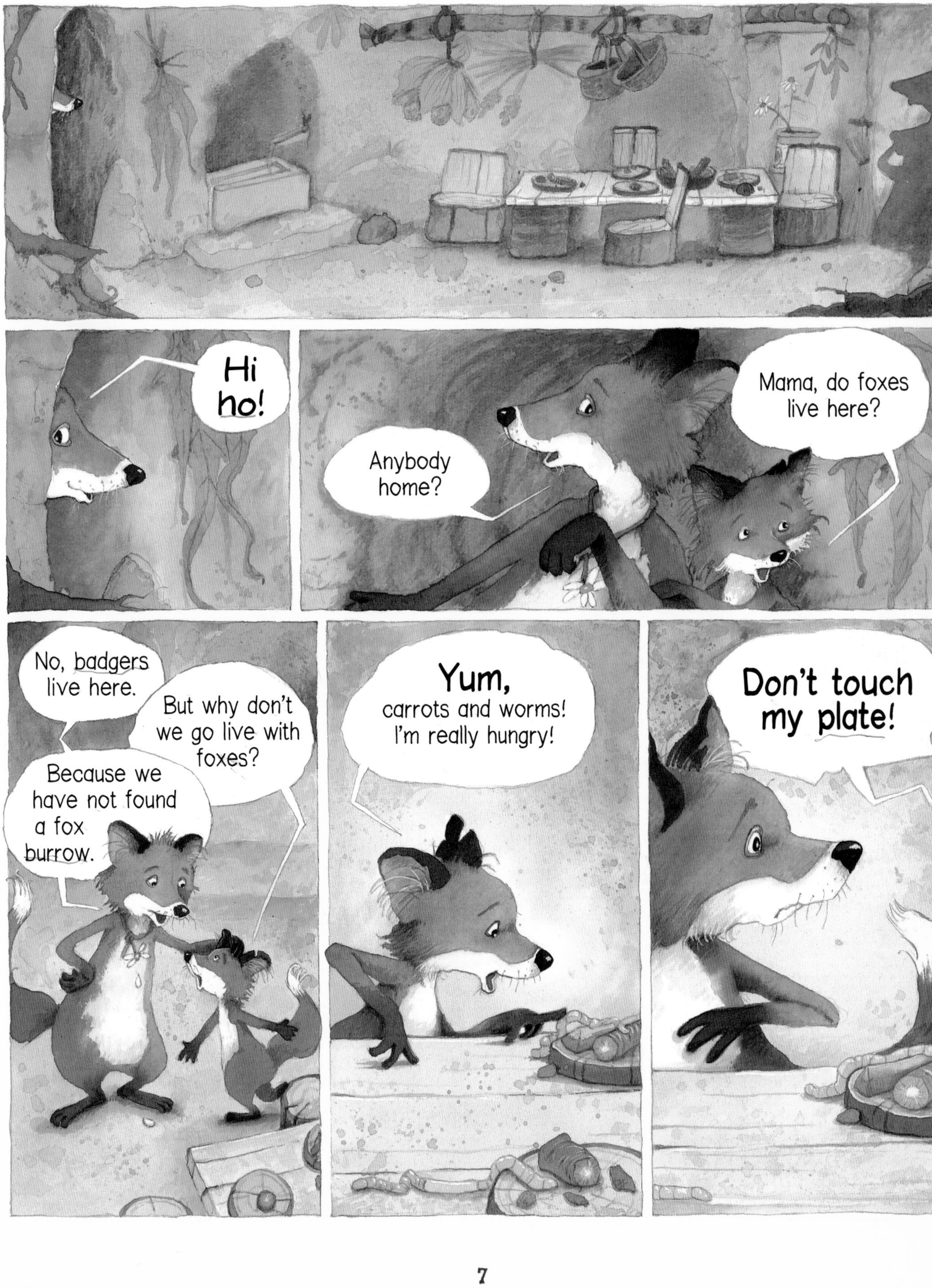

Hi ho!
Anybody home?
Mama, do foxes live here?
No, badgers live here.
But why don't we go live with foxes?
Because we have not found a fox burrow.
Yum, carrots and worms! I'm really hungry!
Don't touch my plate!

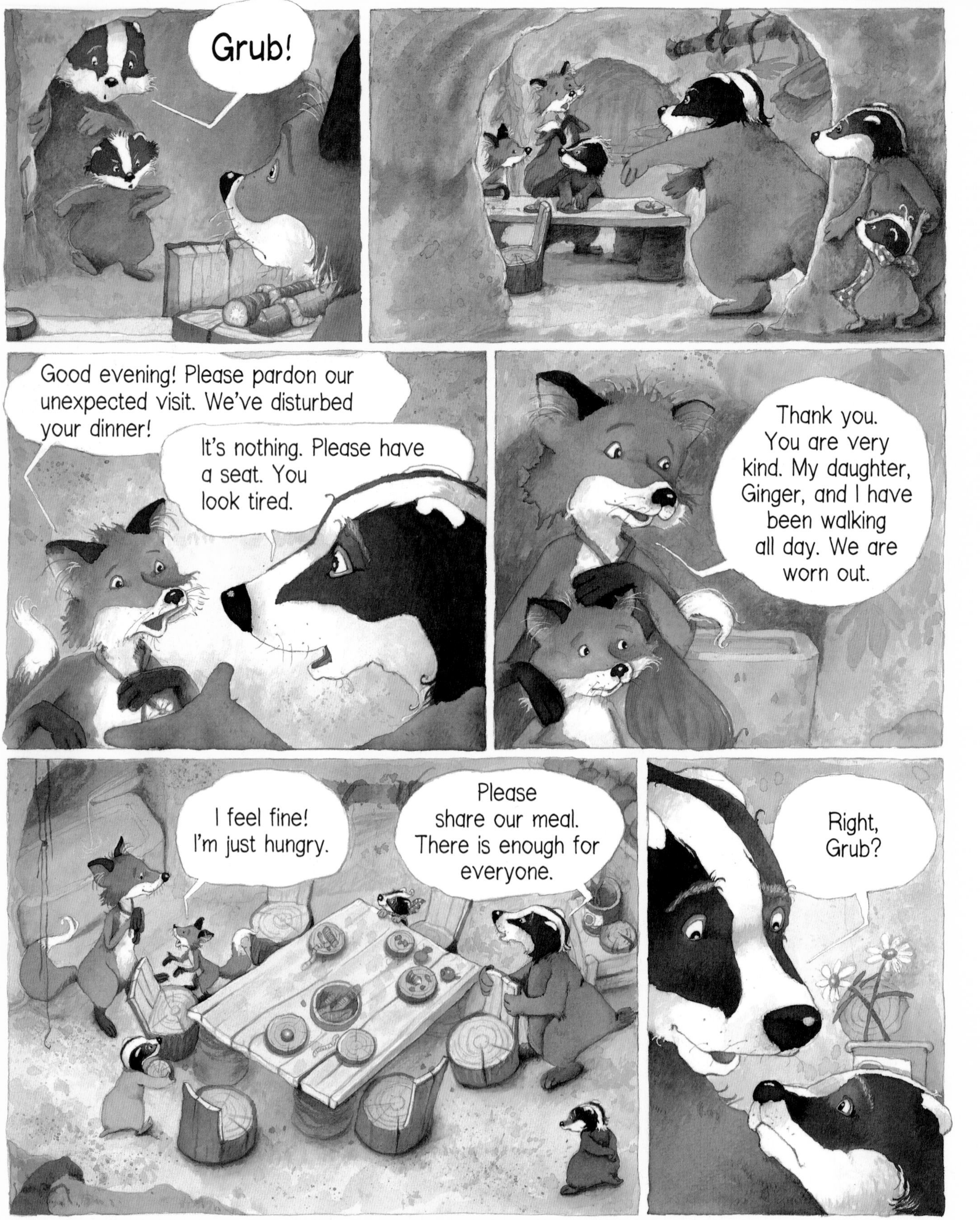
Grub!
Good evening! Please pardon our unexpected visit. We've disturbed your dinner!
It's nothing. Please have a seat. You look tired.
Thank you. You are very kind. My daughter, Ginger, and I have been walking all day. We are worn out.
I feel fine! I'm just hungry.
Please share our meal. There is enough for everyone.
Right, Grub?

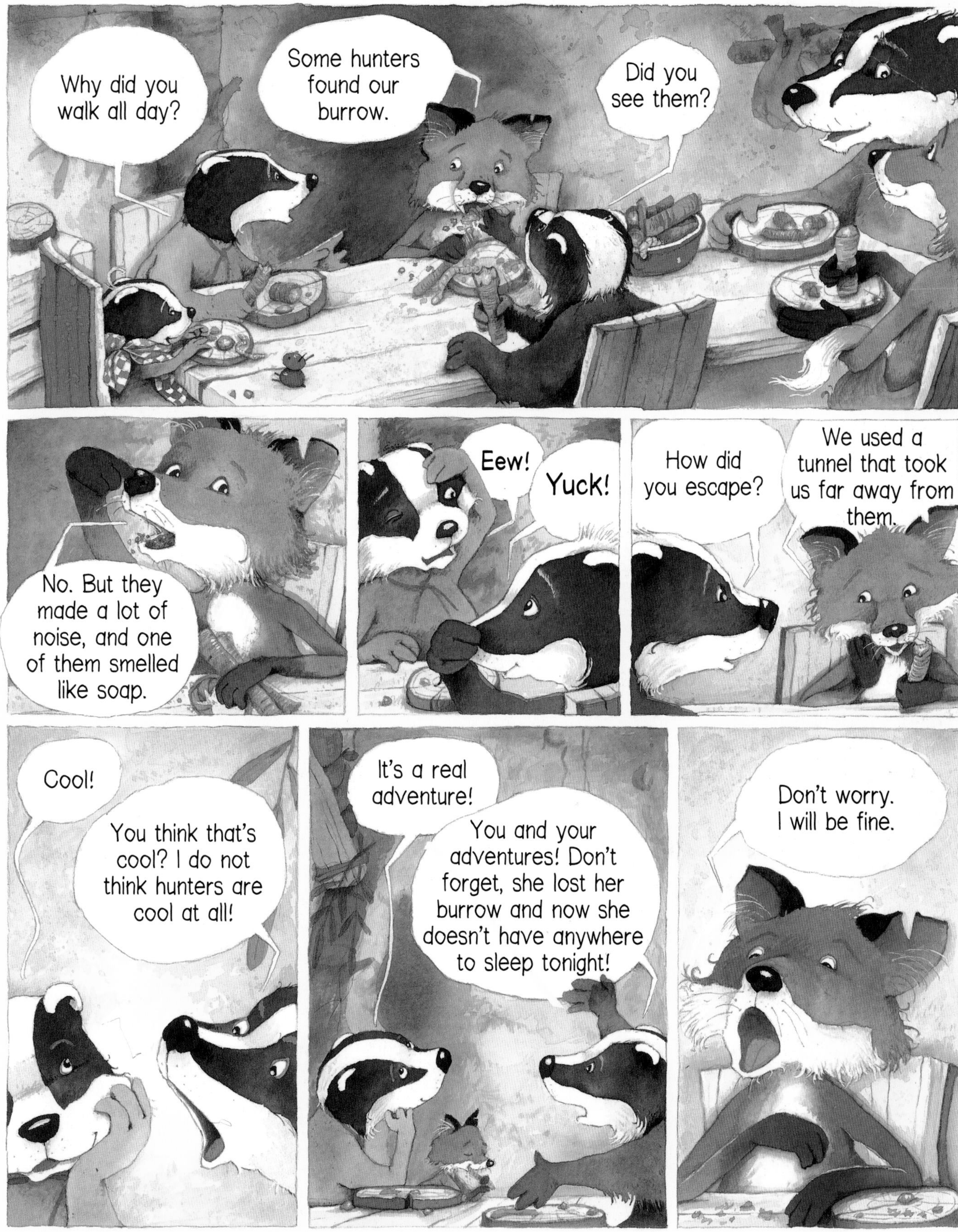
Why did you walk all day?
Some hunters found our burrow.
Did you see them?
No. But they made a lot of noise, and one of them smelled like soap.
Eew!
Yuck!
How did you escape?
We used a tunnel that took us far away from them.
Cool!
You think that's cool? I do not think hunters are cool at all!
It's a real adventure!
You and your adventures! Don't forget, she lost her burrow and now she doesn't have anywhere to sleep tonight!
Don't worry. I will be fine.

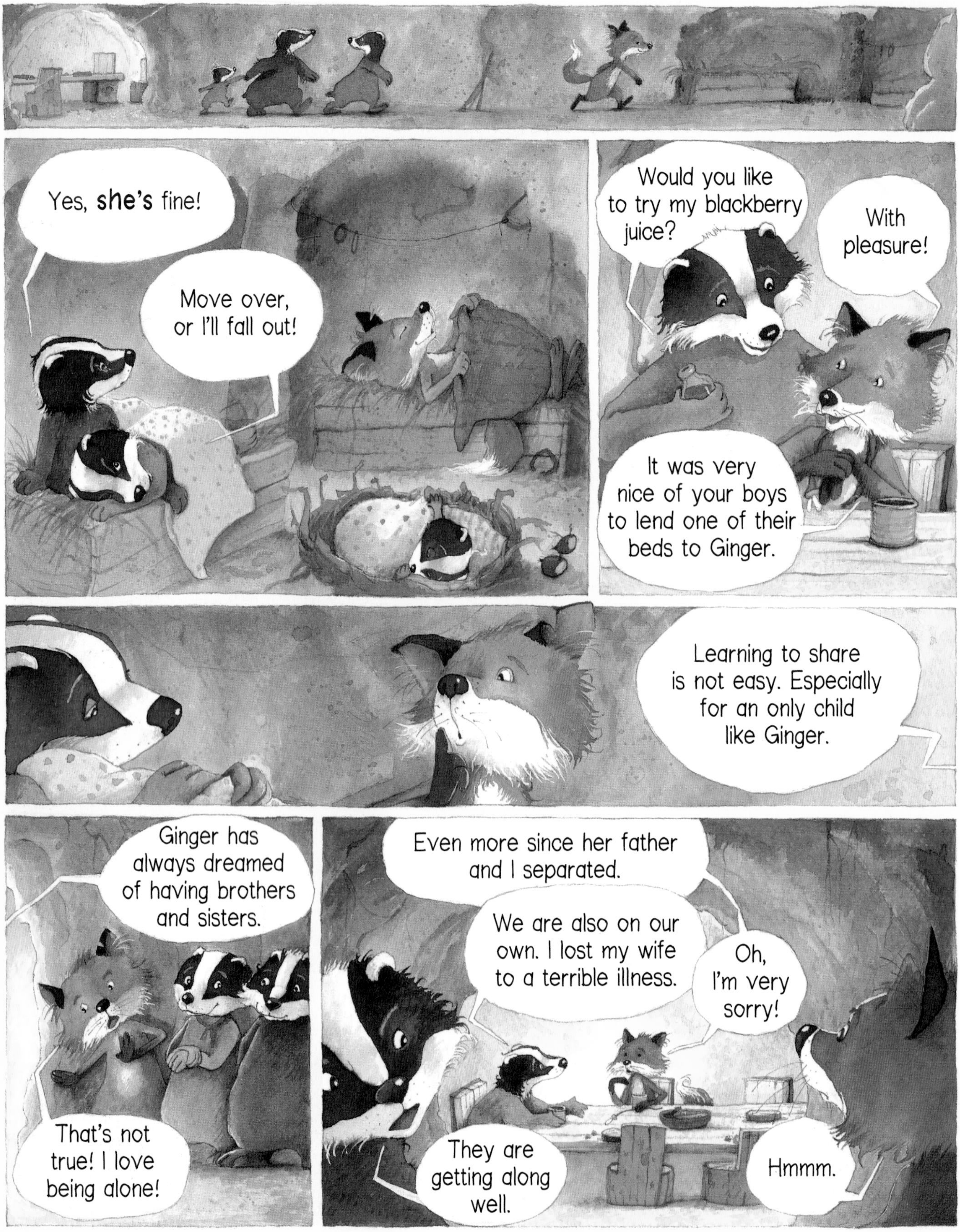
Yes, **she's** fine!
Move over, or I'll fall out!
Would you like to try my blackberry juice?
With pleasure!
It was very nice of your boys to lend one of their beds to Ginger.
Learning to share is not easy. Especially for an only child like Ginger.
Ginger has always dreamed of having brothers and sisters.
That's not true! I love being alone!
Even more since her father and I separated.
We are also on our own. I lost my wife to a terrible illness.
Oh, I'm very sorry!
They are getting along well.
Hmmm.

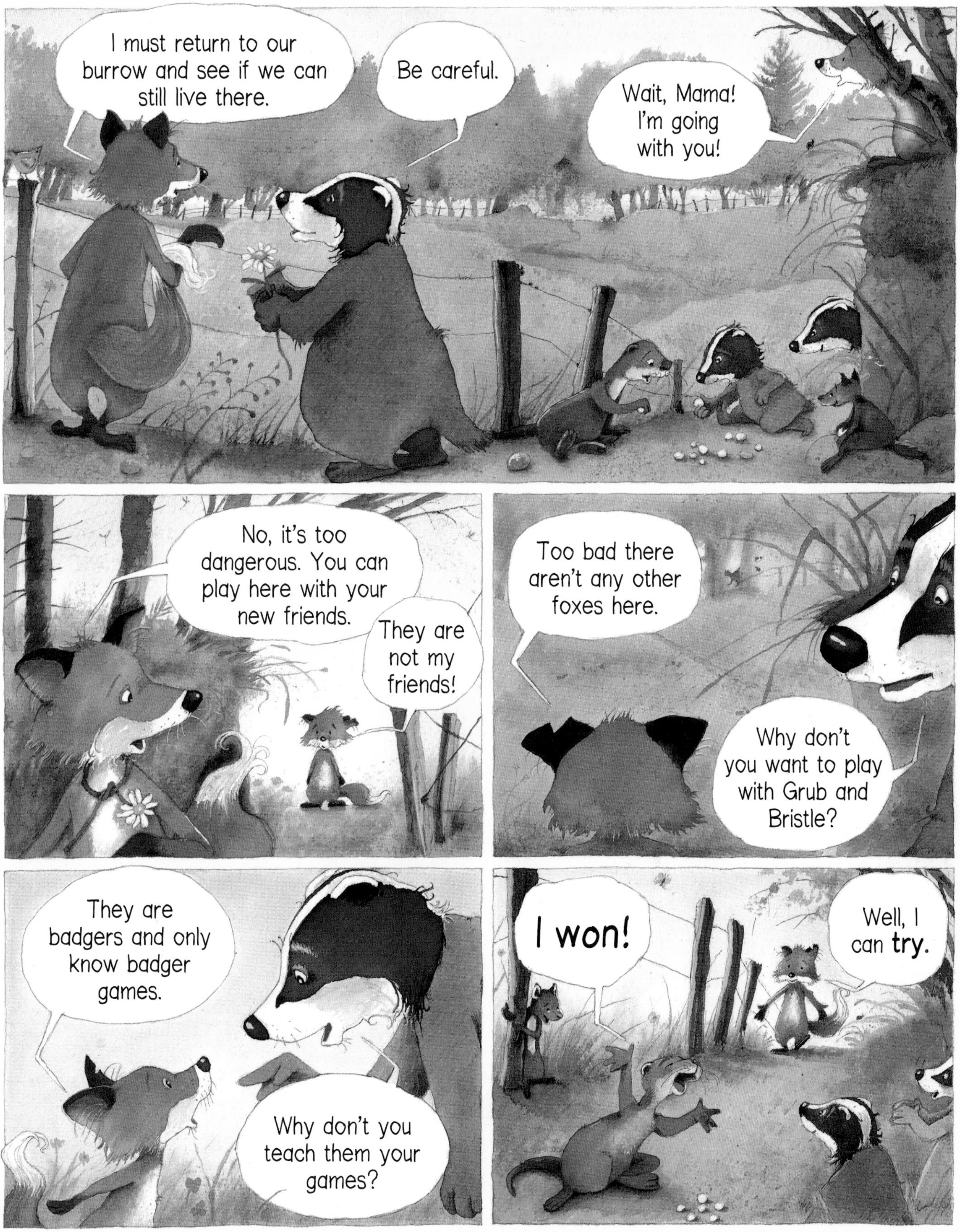
I must return to our burrow and see if we can still live there.
Be careful.
Wait, Mama! I'm going with you!
No, it's too dangerous. You can play here with your new friends.
They are not my friends!
Too bad there aren't any other foxes here.
Why don't you want to play with Grub and Bristle?
They are badgers and only know badger games.
Why don't you teach them your games?
I won!
Well, I can **try**.

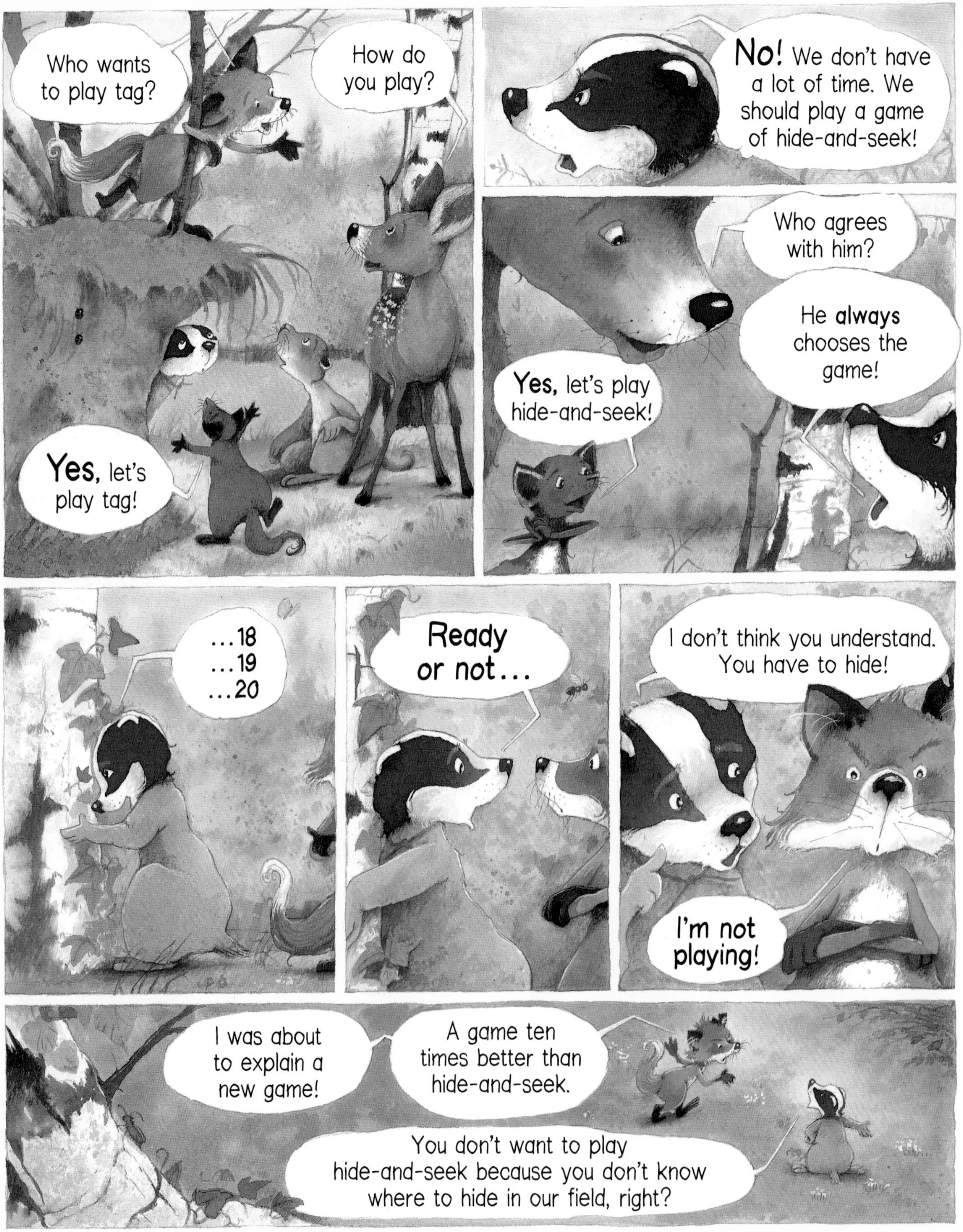
Who wants to play tag?
How do you play?
Yes, let's play tag!
No! We don't have a lot of time. We should play a game of hide-and-seek!
Who agrees with him?
He always chooses the game!
Yes, let's play hide-and-seek!
...18 ...19 ...20
Ready or not...
I don't think you understand. You have to hide!
I'm not playing!
I was about to explain a new game!
A game ten times better than hide-and-seek.
You don't want to play hide-and-seek because you don't know where to hide in our field, right?

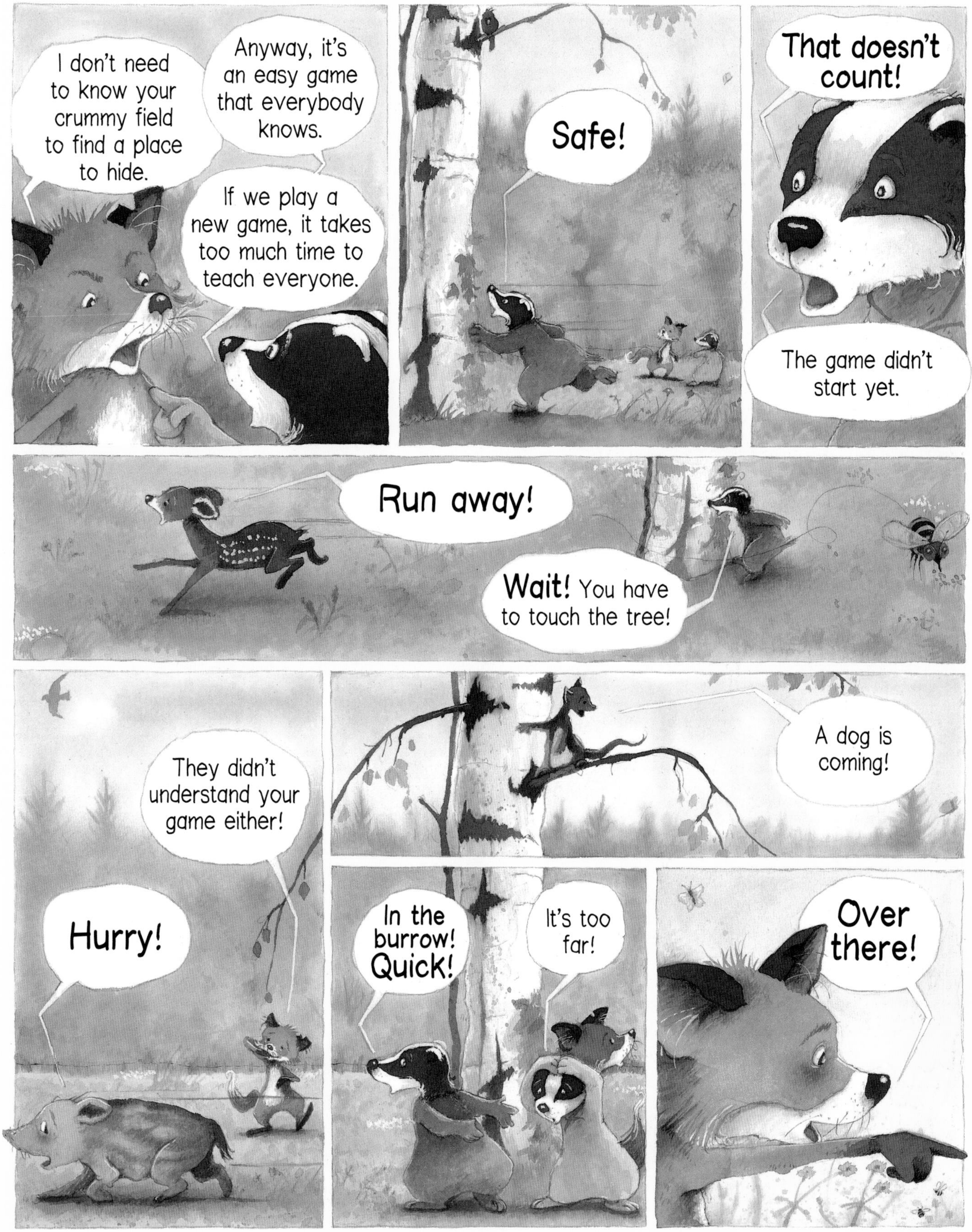

I don't need to know your crummy field to find a place to hide.
Anyway, it's an easy game that everybody knows.
If we play a new game, it takes too much time to teach everyone.
Safe!
That doesn't count!
The game didn't start yet.
Run away!
Wait! You have to touch the tree!
They didn't understand your game either!
Hurry!
A dog is coming!
In the burrow! Quick!
It's too far!
Over there!

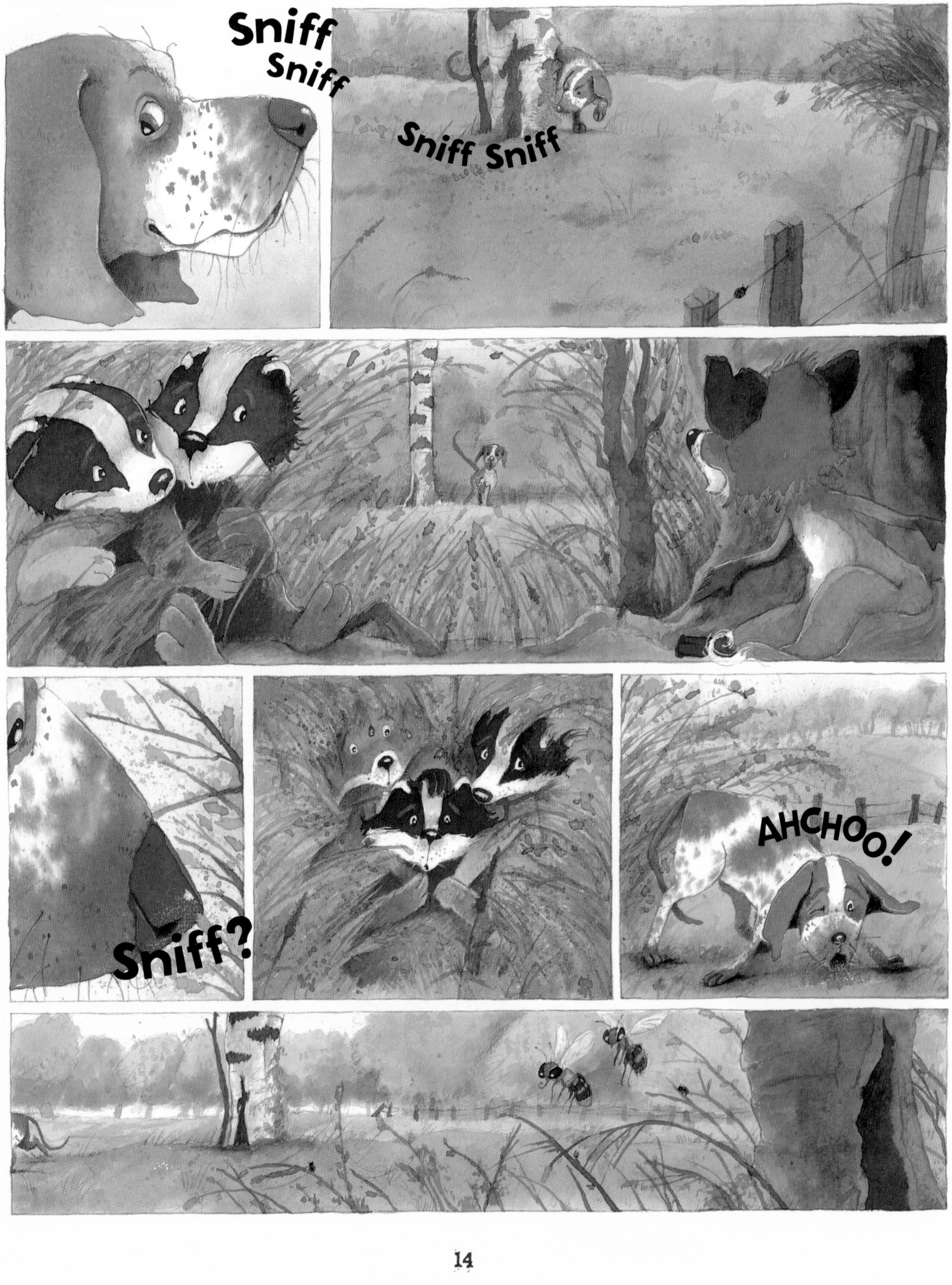
Sniff
Sniff
Sniff Sniff
Sniff?
AHCHOO!

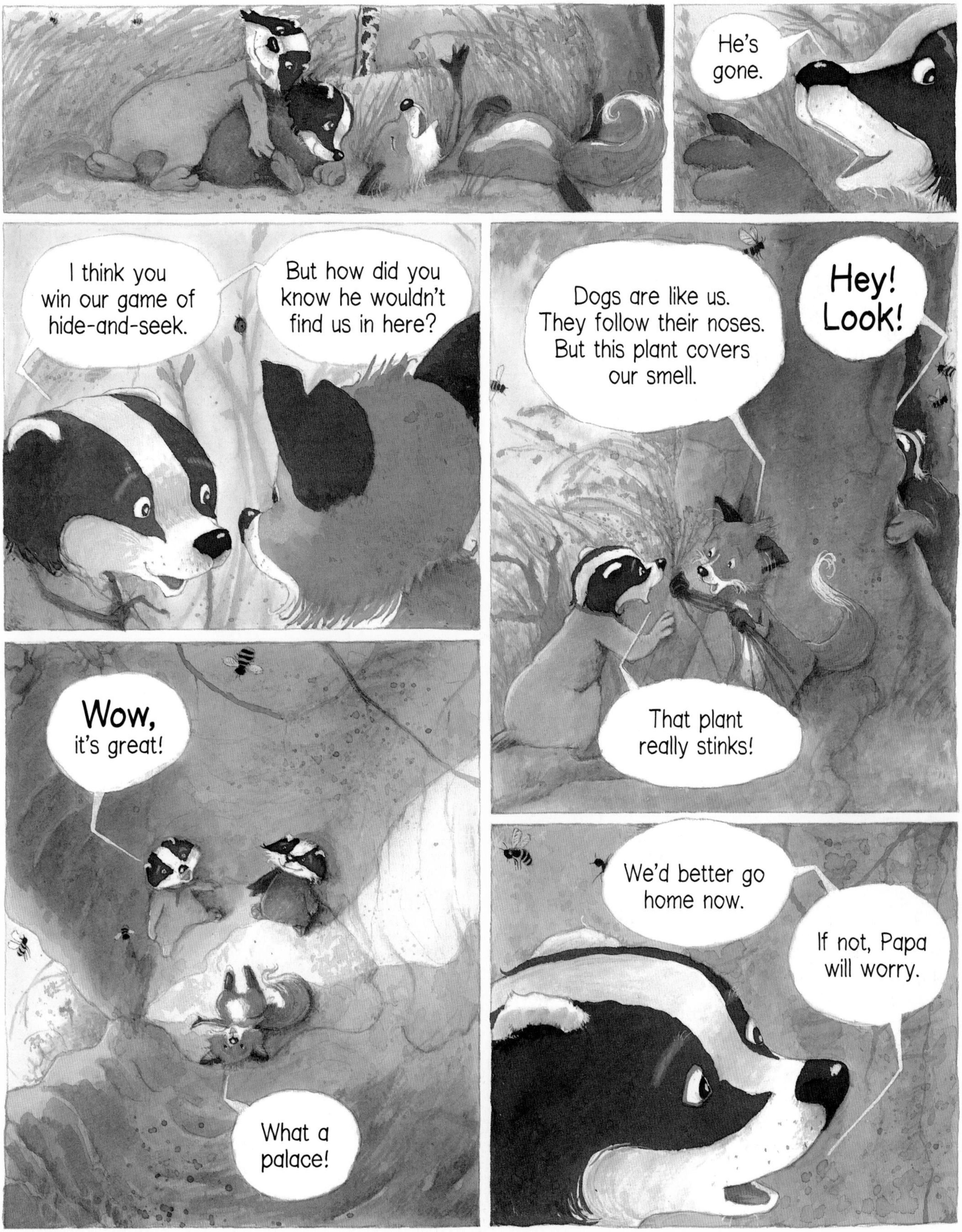
He's gone.
I think you win our game of hide-and-seek.
But how did you know he wouldn't find us in here?
Dogs are like us. They follow their noses. But this plant covers our smell.
Hey! Look!
That plant really stinks!
Wow, it's great!
What a palace!
We'd better go home now.
If not, Papa will worry.

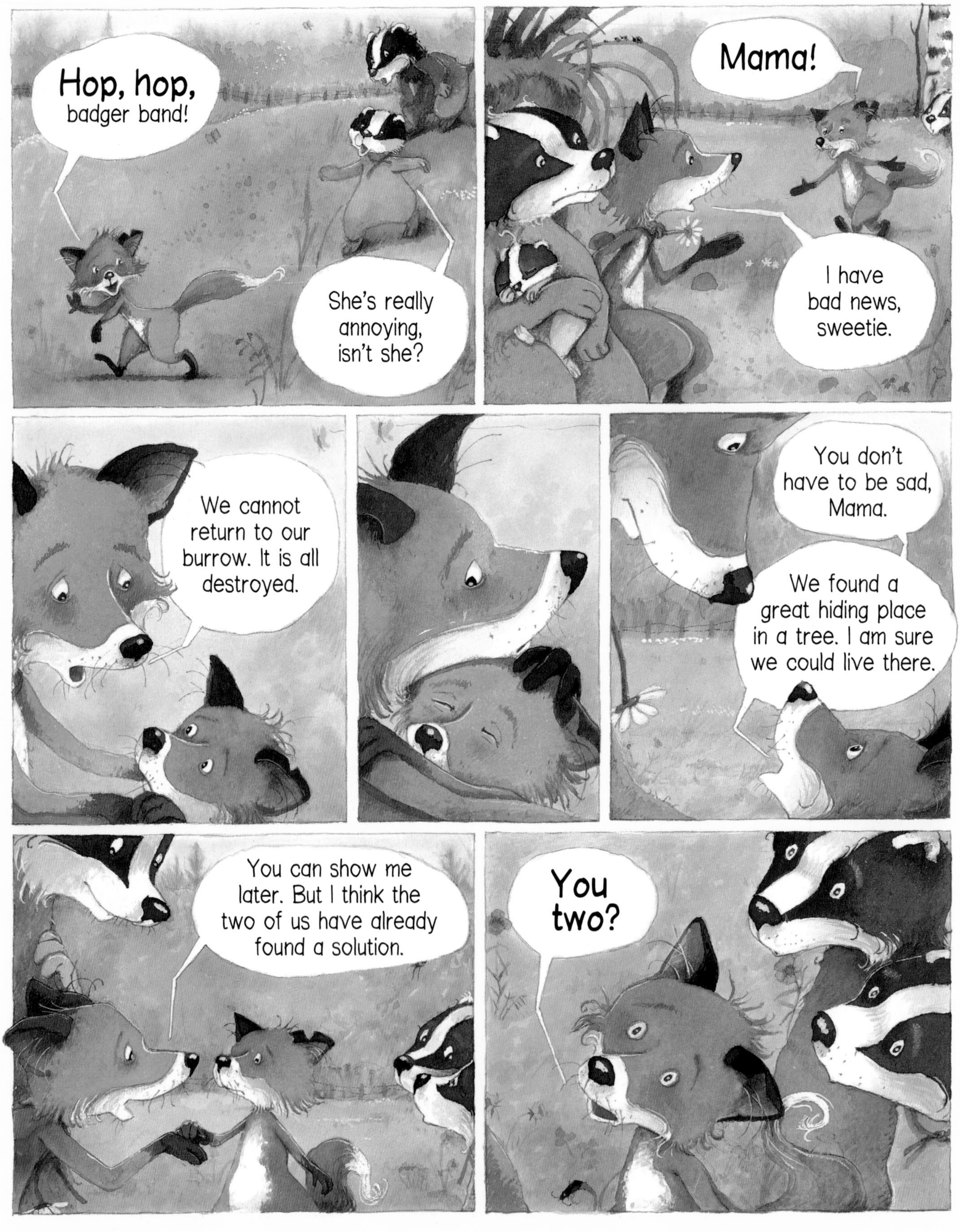
Hop, hop, badger band!
She's really annoying, isn't she?
Mama!
I have bad news, sweetie.
We cannot return to our burrow. It is all destroyed.
You don't have to be sad, Mama.
We found a great hiding place in a tree. I am sure we could live there.
You can show me later. But I think the two of us have already found a solution.
You two?

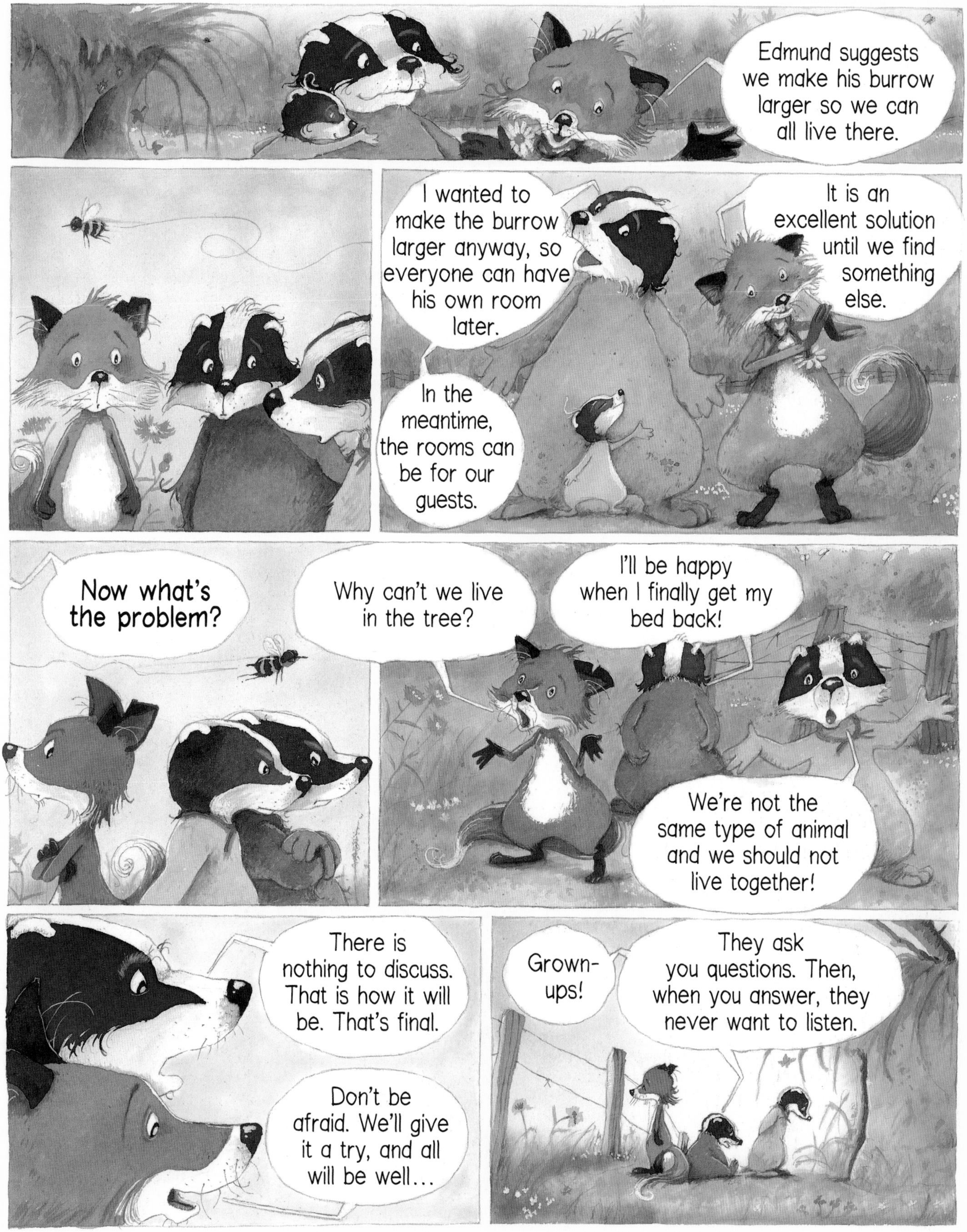
Edmund suggests we make his burrow larger so we can all live there.
I wanted to make the burrow larger anyway, so everyone can have his own room later.
In the meantime, the rooms can be for our guests.
It is an excellent solution until we find something else.
Now what's the problem?
Why can't we live in the tree?
I'll be happy when I finally get my bed back!
We're not the same type of animal and we should not live together!
There is nothing to discuss. That is how it will be. That's final.
Don't be afraid. We'll give it a try, and all will be well…
Grown-ups!
They ask you questions. Then, when you answer, they never want to listen.

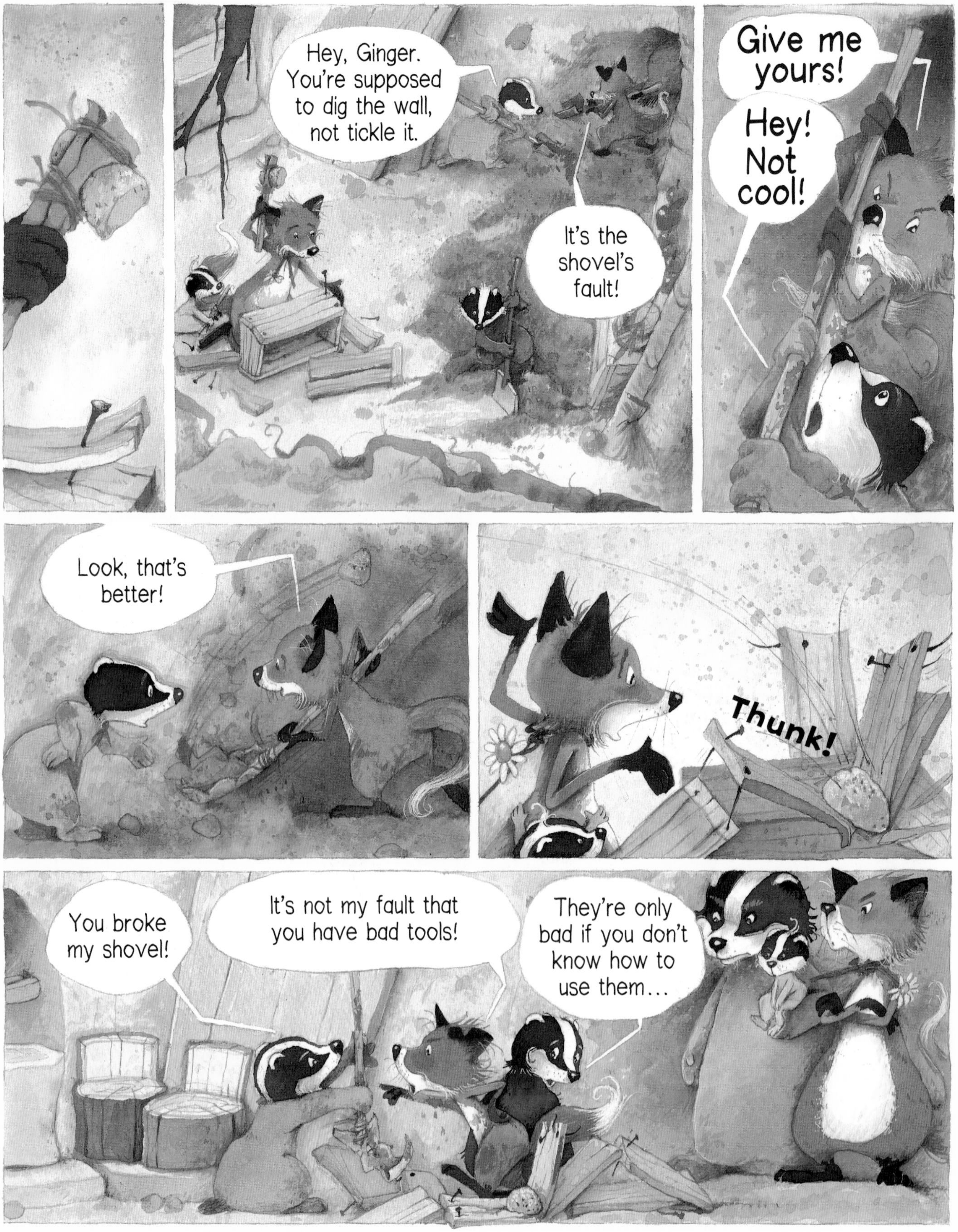
Hey, Ginger. You're supposed to dig the wall, not tickle it.
It's the shovel's fault!
Give me yours!
Hey! Not cool!
Look, that's better!
Thunk!
You broke my shovel!
It's not my fault that you have bad tools!
They're only bad if you don't know how to use them...

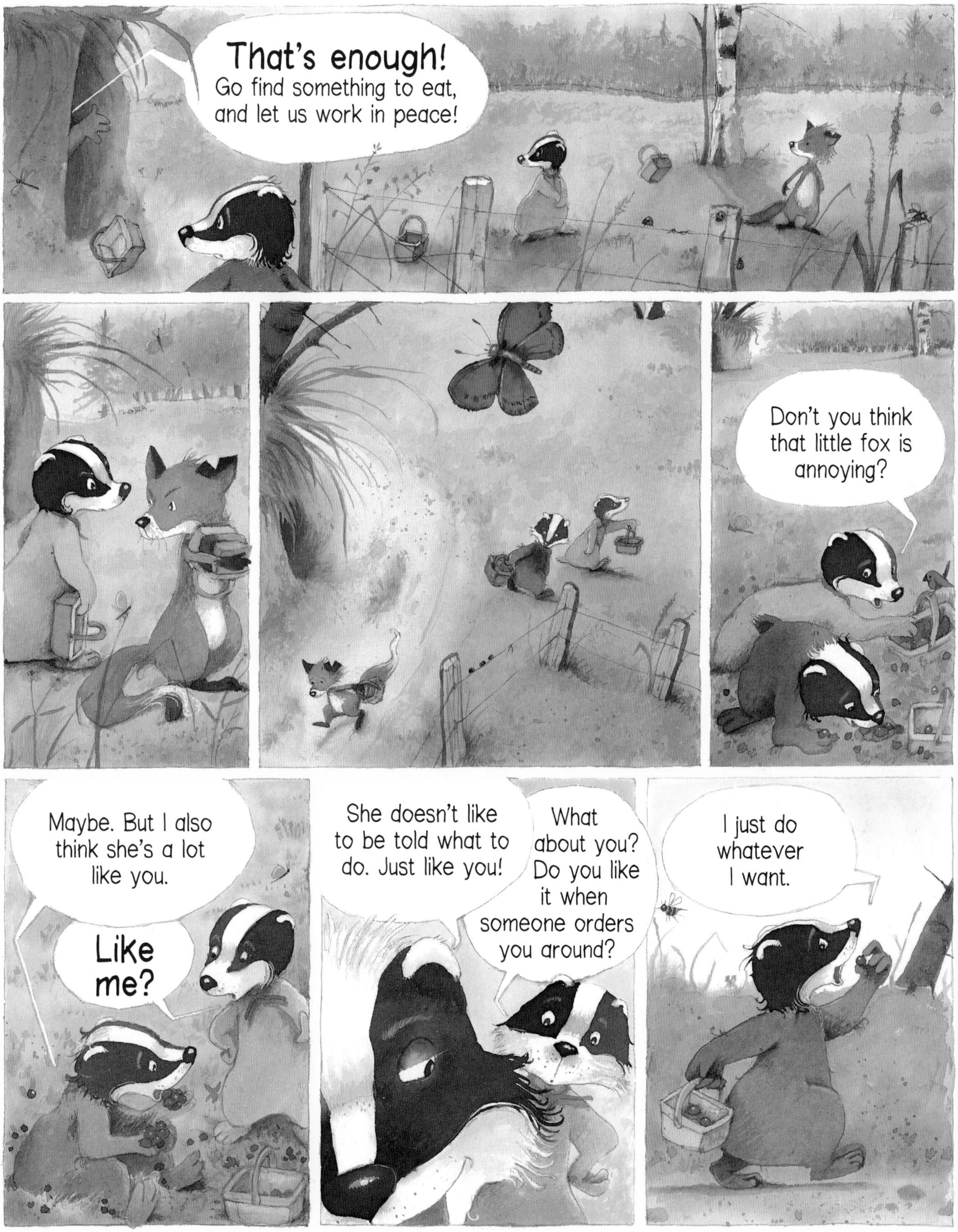
That's enough! Go find something to eat, and let us work in peace!
Don't you think that little fox is annoying?
Maybe. But I also think she's a lot like you.
Like me?
She doesn't like to be told what to do. Just like you!
What about you? Do you like it when someone orders you around?
I just do whatever I want.

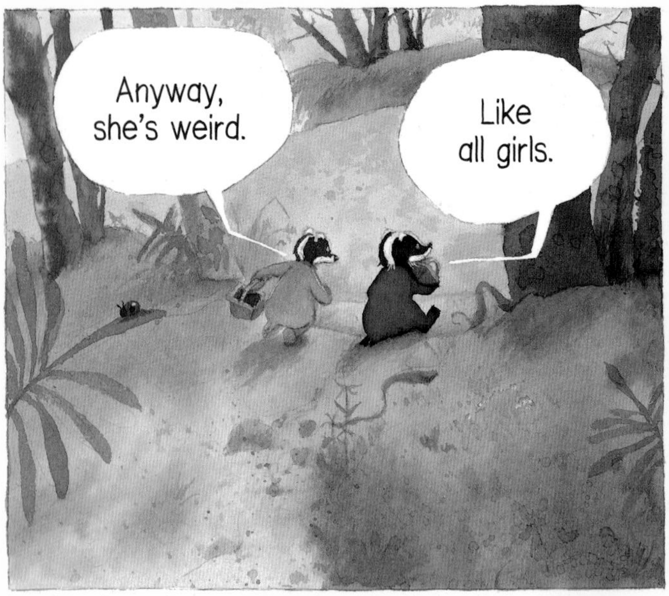
Anyway, she's weird.
Like all girls.

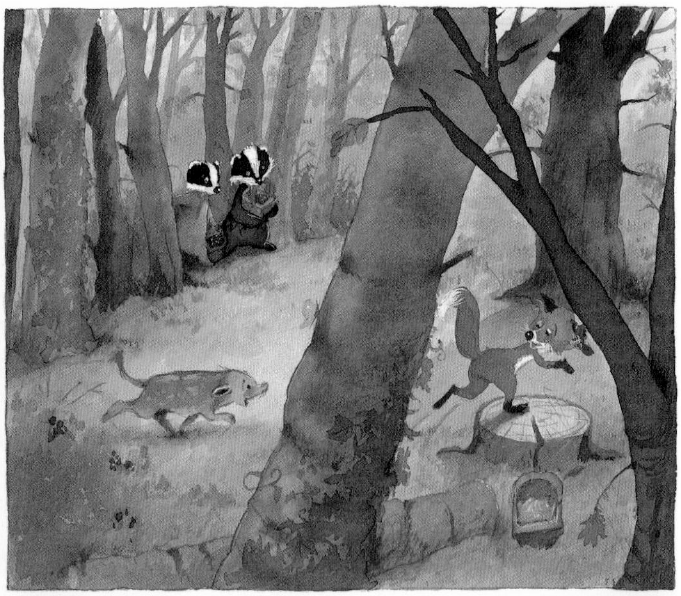

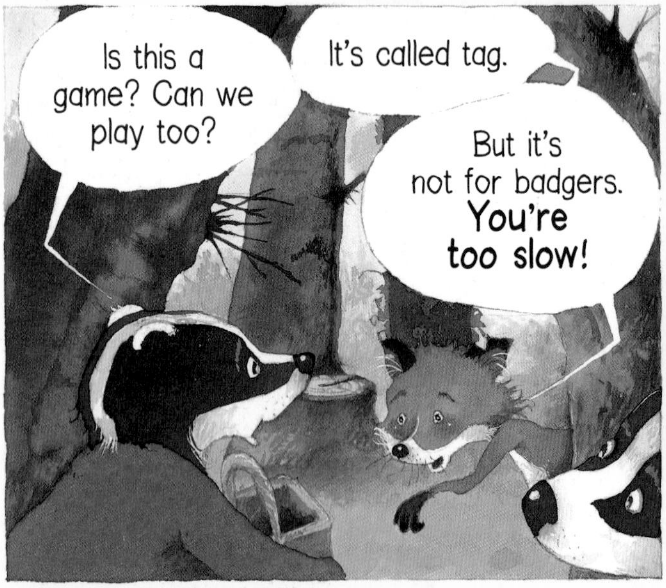
Is this a game? Can we play too?
It's called tag.
But it's not for badgers. **You're too slow!**

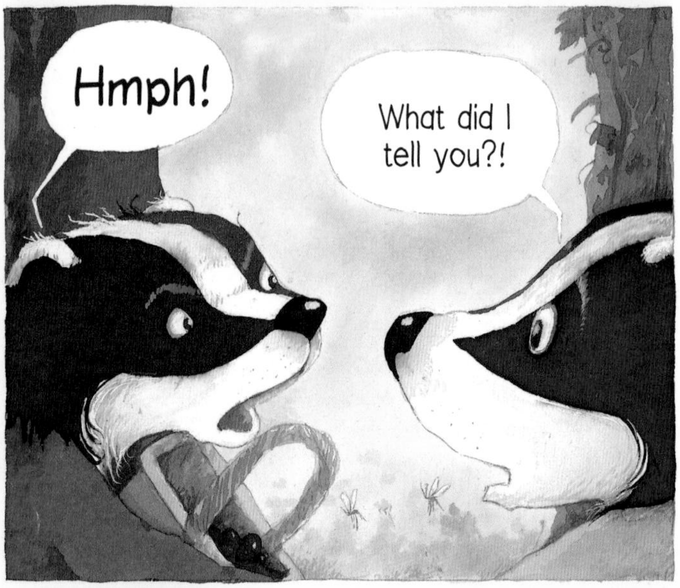
Hmph!
What did I tell you?!

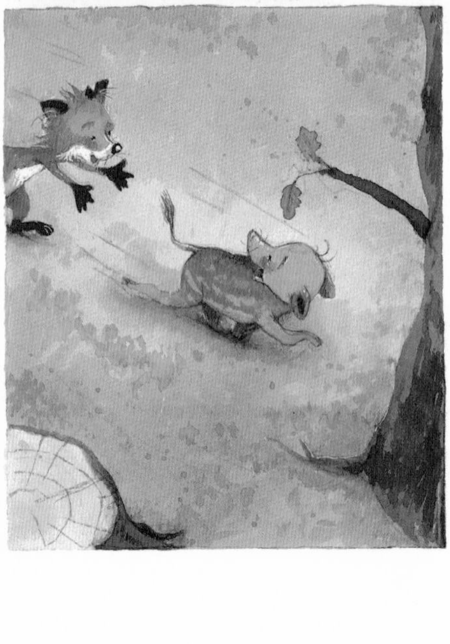

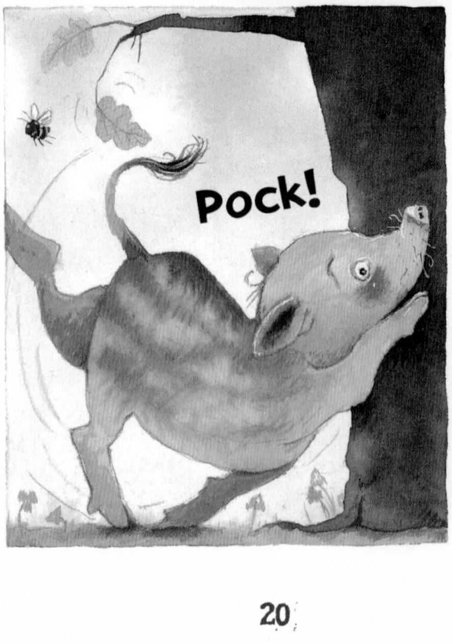
Pock!

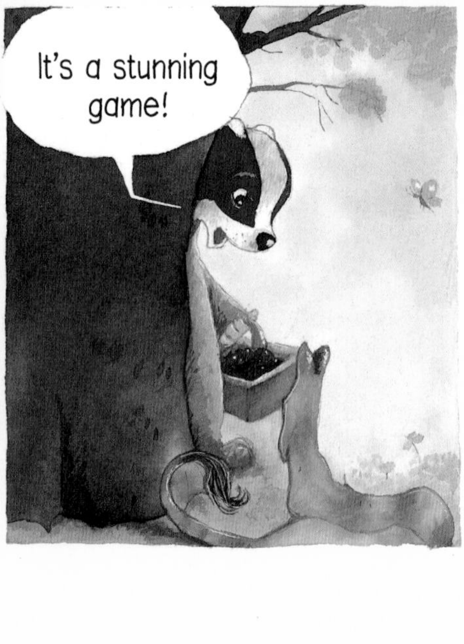
It's a stunning game!

Stop joking, he's hurt!
And how is that **my** fault?
Ow
Stop it, you two!
We have to make a stretcher and take him home!
Ownk
It's **too heavy!**
What happened?
You ran a little too fast in Ginger's game.
Ok, that's enough, Bristle. Don't exaggerate. I get it.
Oh yes? Then explain it. What do you understand?

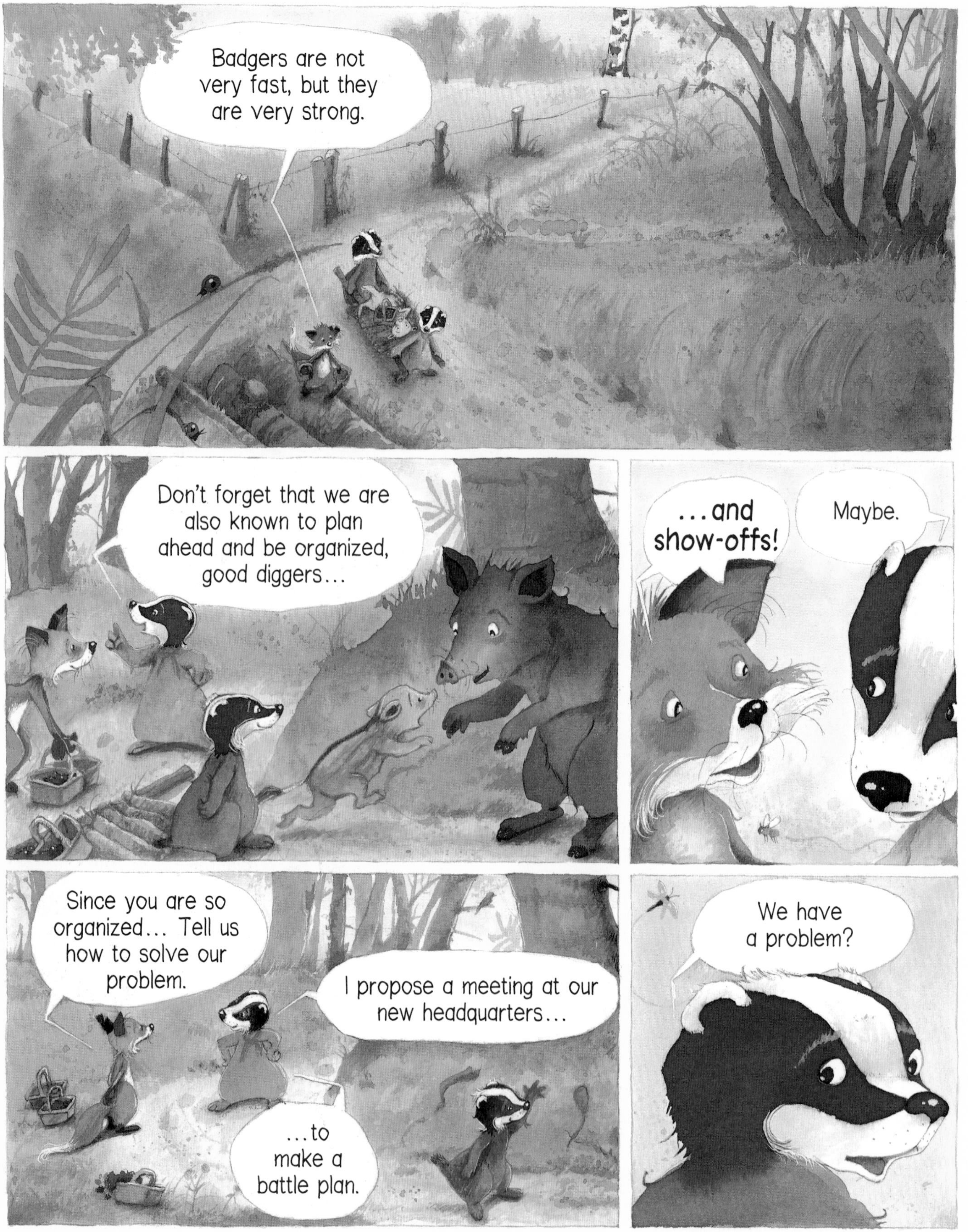
Badgers are not very fast, but they are very strong.
Don't forget that we are also known to plan ahead and be organized, good diggers...
...and show-offs!
Maybe.
Since you are so organized... Tell us how to solve our problem.
I propose a meeting at our new headquarters...
...to make a battle plan.
We have a problem?

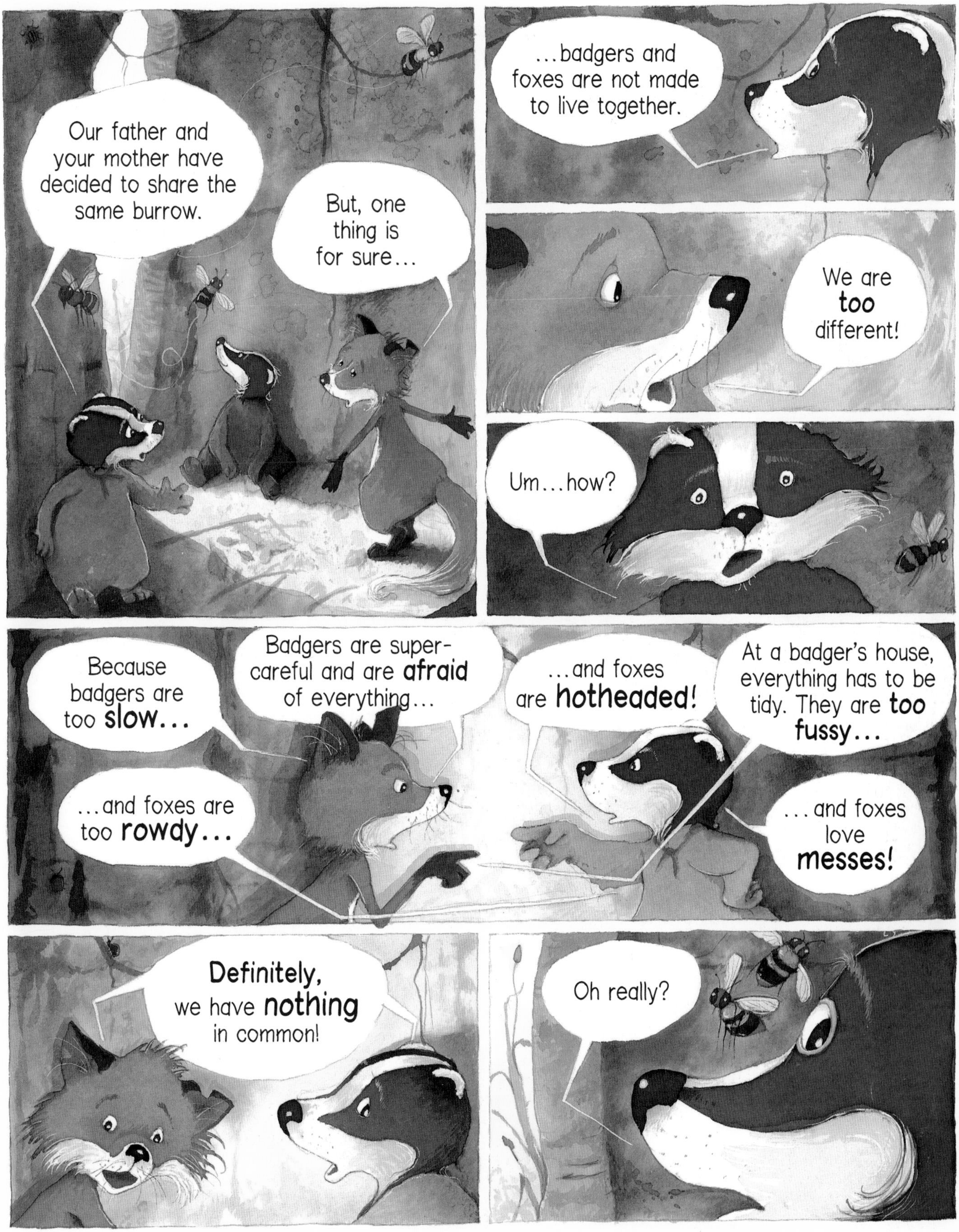
Our father and your mother have decided to share the same burrow.
But, one thing is for sure...
...badgers and foxes are not made to live together.
We are too different!
Um...how?
Because badgers are too slow...
Badgers are super-careful and are afraid of everything...
...and foxes are too rowdy...
...and foxes are hotheaded!
At a badger's house, everything has to be tidy. They are too fussy...
...and foxes love messes!
Definitely, we have nothing in common!
Oh really?

But our father doesn't see that.

And my mother doesn't see it.

So, we have to help them see it clearly.

Hey, come here!

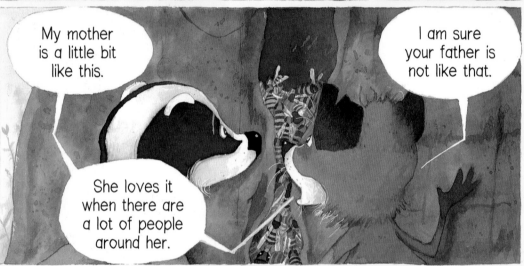

My mother is a little bit like this.

She loves it when there are a lot of people around her.

I am sure your father is not like that.

He likes peace and quiet, that's for sure.

What if we organize an **enormous** party for them both?

That's the solution!

Our father will see that this fox is too tiring for him.

And my mother will understand that she cannot live with a party pooper badger!

True. A party is never a bad idea.

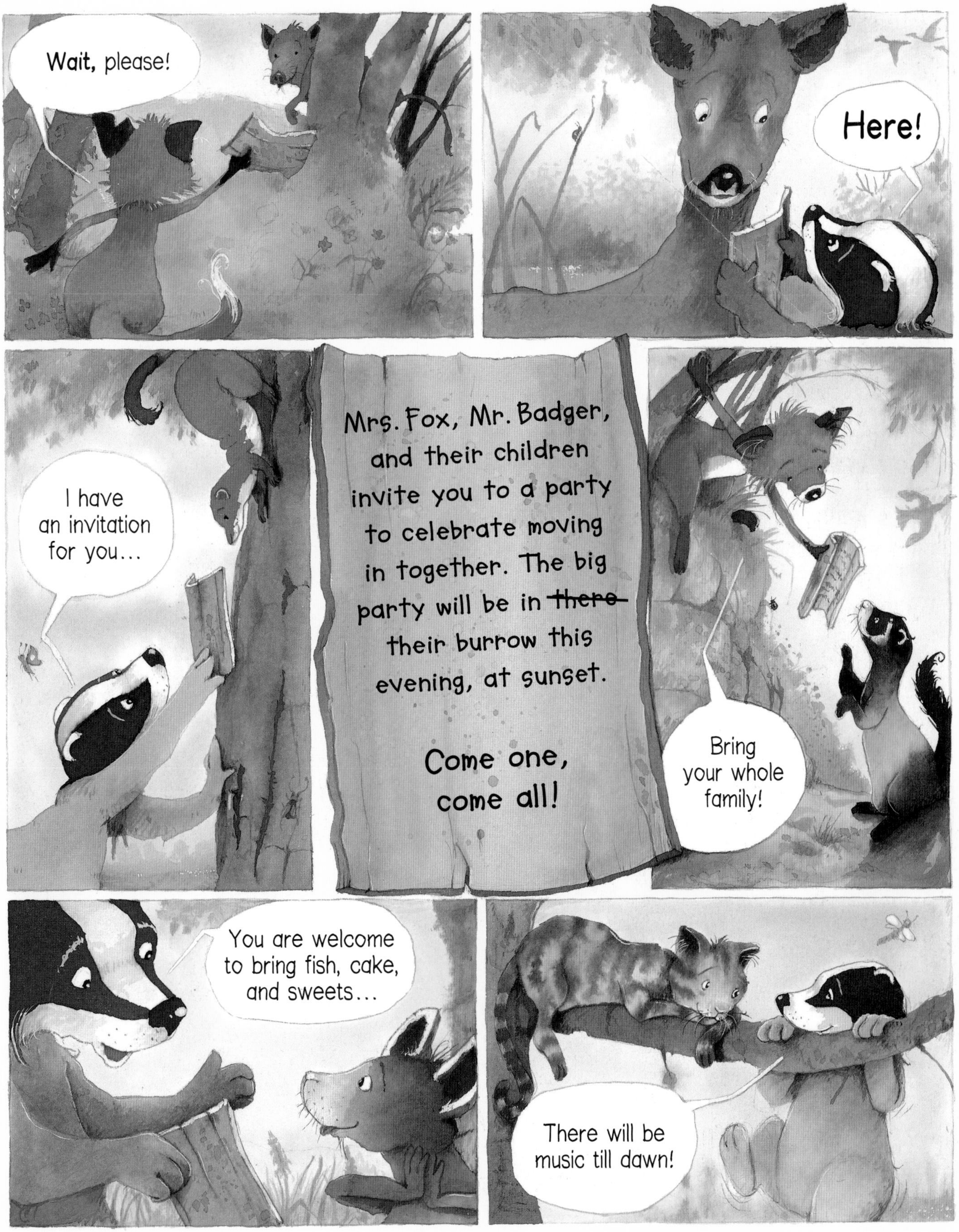
Wait, please!
Here!
I have an invitation for you...
Mrs. Fox, Mr. Badger, and their children invite you to a party to celebrate moving in together. The big party will be in ~~there~~ their burrow this evening, at sunset.
Come one, come all!
Bring your whole family!
You are welcome to bring fish, cake, and sweets...
There will be music till dawn!

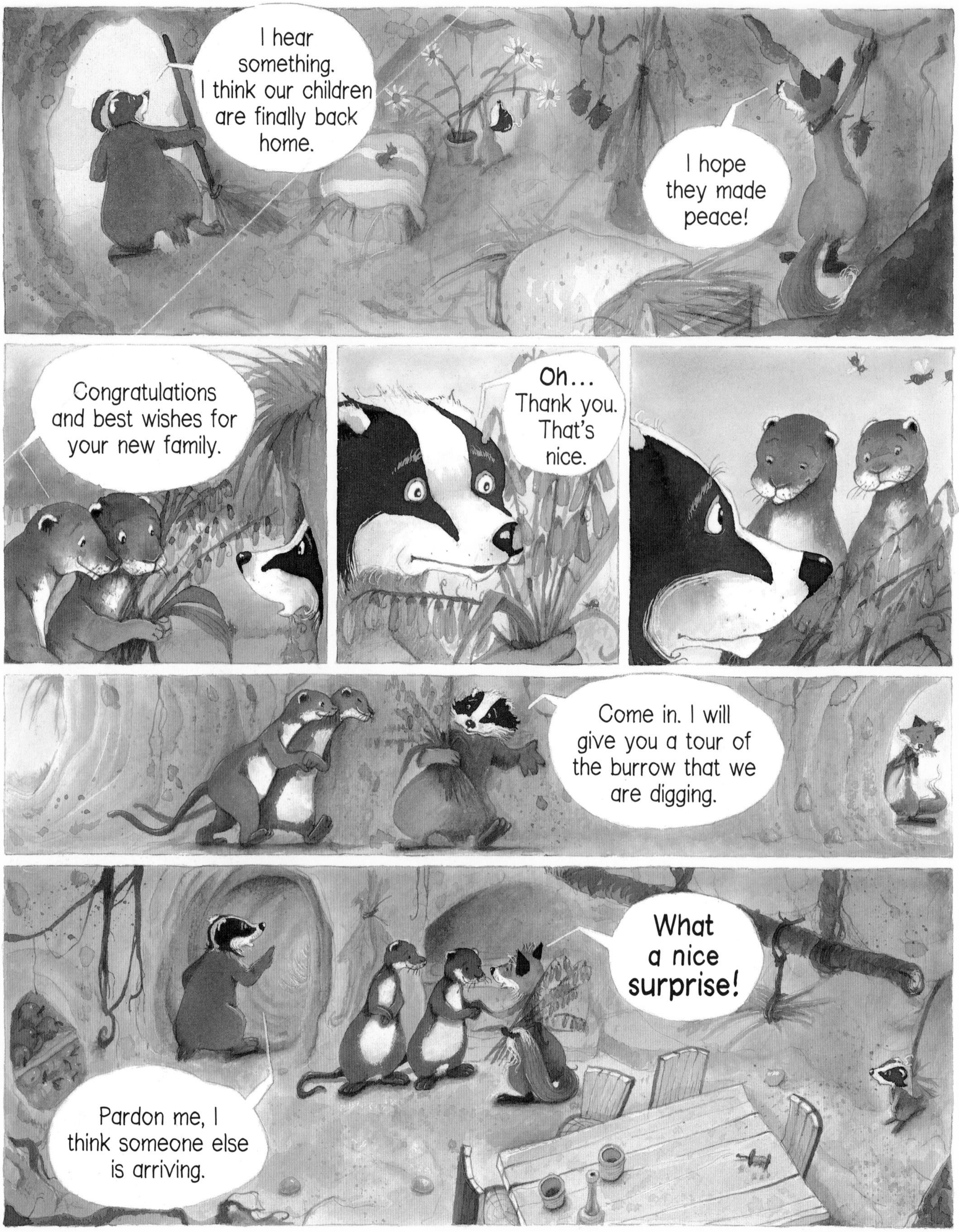
I hear something. I think our children are finally back home.
I hope they made peace!
Congratulations and best wishes for your new family.
Oh... Thank you. That's nice.
Come in. I will give you a tour of the burrow that we are digging.
What a nice surprise!
Pardon me, I think someone else is arriving.

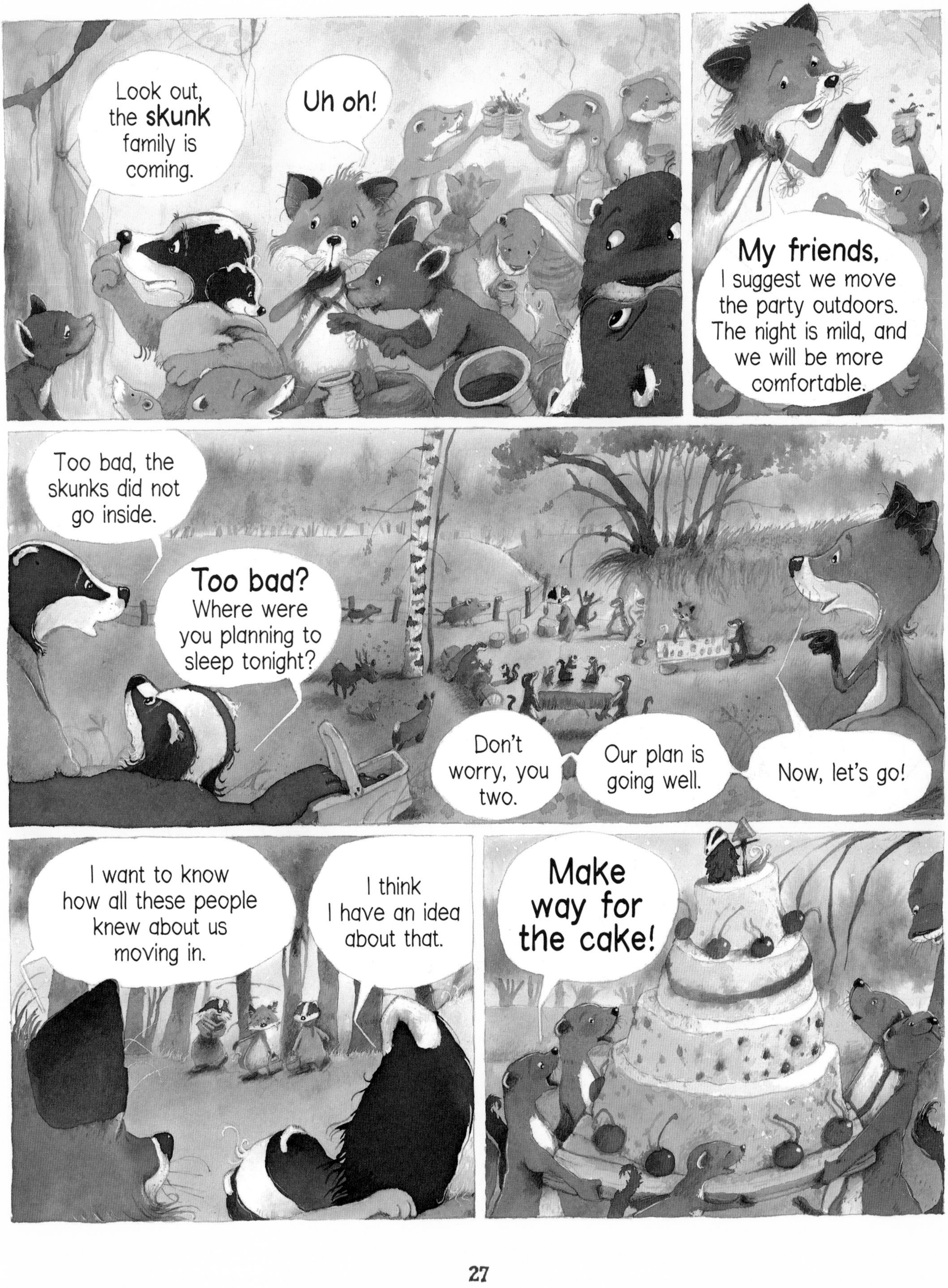
Look out, the skunk family is coming.
Uh oh!
My friends, I suggest we move the party outdoors. The night is mild, and we will be more comfortable.
Too bad, the skunks did not go inside.
Too bad? Where were you planning to sleep tonight?
Don't worry, you two.
Our plan is going well.
Now, let's go!
I want to know how all these people knew about us moving in.
I think I have an idea about that.
Make way for the cake!

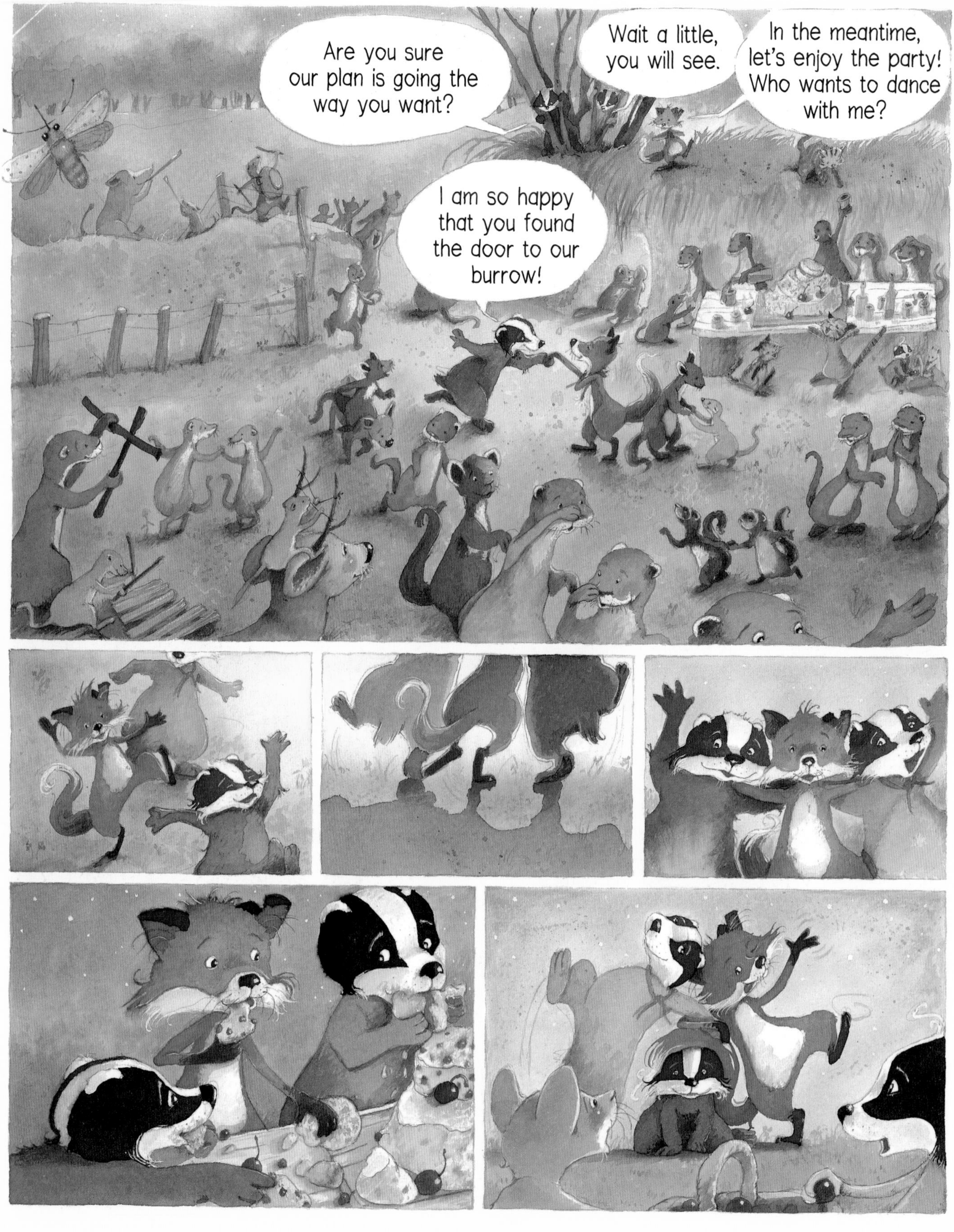
Are you sure our plan is going the way you want?
Wait a little, you will see.
In the meantime, let's enjoy the party! Who wants to dance with me?
I am so happy that you found the door to our burrow!

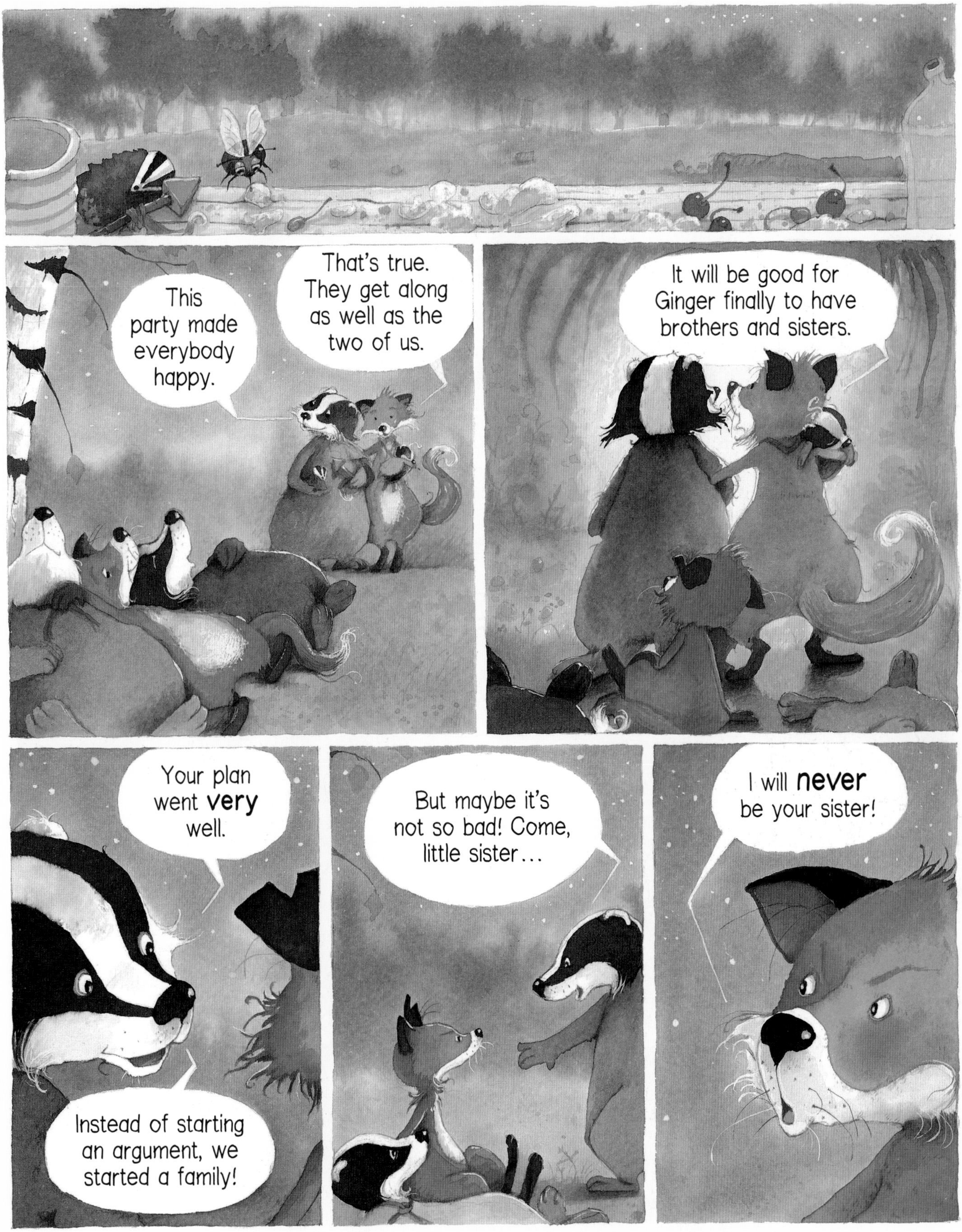
This party made everybody happy.
That's true. They get along as well as the two of us.
It will be good for Ginger finally to have brothers and sisters.
Your plan went **very** well.
Instead of starting an argument, we started a family!
But maybe it's not so bad! Come, little sister...
I will **never** be your sister!

I am a fox and I do not want to **keep stepping over** these slow **badgers** in my house!

Good morning, sweetie!

That was truly a marvelous party that all of you organized.

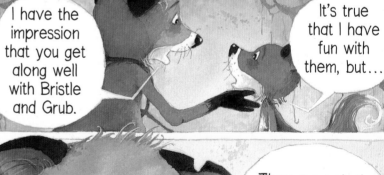

I have the impression that you get along well with Bristle and Grub.

It's true that I have fun with them, but...

They are not at all how I imagined my brothers would be.

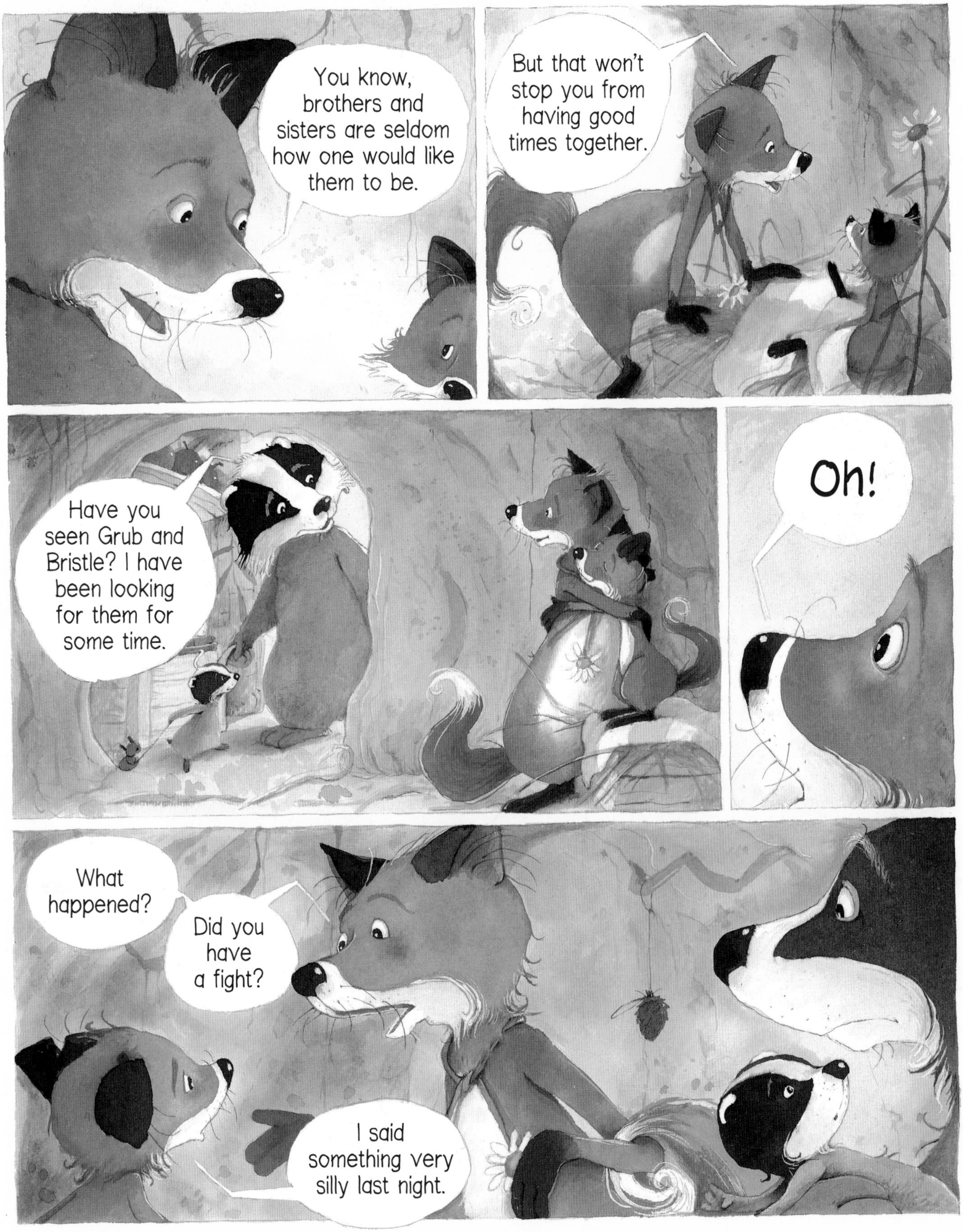
You know, brothers and sisters are seldom how one would like them to be.
But that won't stop you from having good times together.
Have you seen Grub and Bristle? I have been looking for them for some time.
Oh!
What happened?
Did you have a fight?
I said something very silly last night.

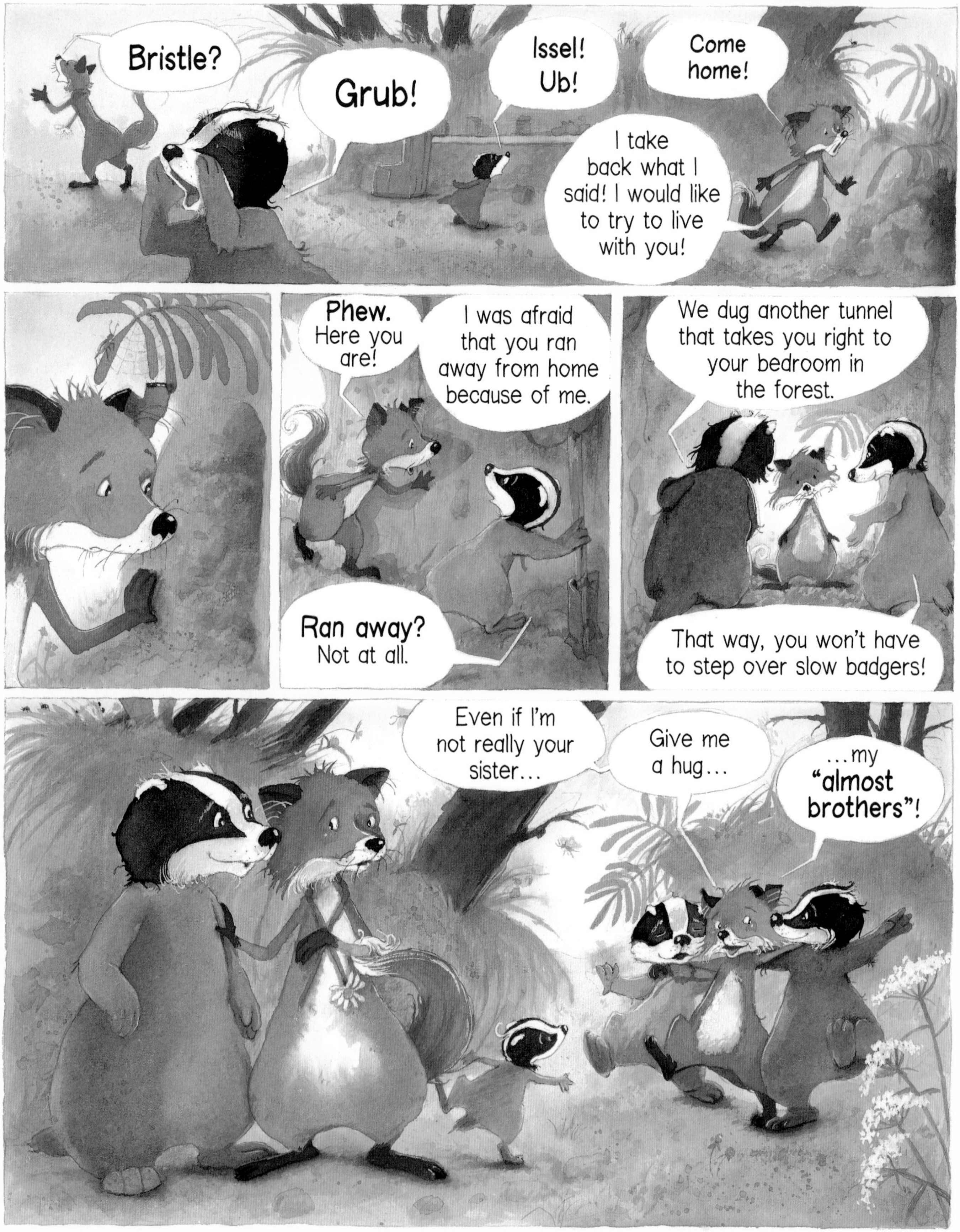
Bristle?
Grub!
Issel! Ub!
Come home!
I take back what I said! I would like to try to live with you!
Phew. Here you are!
I was afraid that you ran away from home because of me.
Ran away? Not at all.
We dug another tunnel that takes you right to your bedroom in the forest.
That way, you won't have to step over slow badgers!
Even if I'm not really your sister...
Give me a hug...
...my "almost brothers"!